# How I intend to get mommy married
## by Danny Gallagher (age 11)

1) Enter the contest Mom's matchmaking service is running—but use a different name 'cause she'd yell at me if she knew I was trying to win her a date for Mother's Day.

2) Once I win the contest, using the name Tommy Smith, fill out the dating questionnaire just like Mom would, but use the name Mary Smith.

3) I find out who Mom's dream date would be, which I just know is gonna be Chris Maverick, then make sure me and Mom just happen to be where Chris and "Mary" are supposed to meet for their blind date.

4) Then, while we all wait for the mysterious Mary Smith to show up, show them how right for each other they are!

5) If all else fails, run away to the nearest wedding chapel!

*Dear Reader,*

What to give the World's Best Mom for Mother's Day? Every year I try to come up with something really special. If my mom wasn't already married, I just might steal little Danny Gallagher's gift idea in Marie Ferrarella's *Let's Get Mommy Married*. Danny decides to surprise his happily *un*married mom with a date for Mother's Day. Then, Mom will have a husband, Danny will have a dad...and maybe a couple of baby brothers and sisters....

Speaking of mothers and marriage—ever thought a mother hen would come in the form of a tall, dark and incredibly gorgeous Marine? In Jo Ann Algermissen's *I Do?*, Max O'Roarke marches into the Bridal Bliss boutique and orders owner Amy Brantley to cancel his baby sister's wedding gown. But Amy's too busy sizing him for a tuxedo he can get double use out of....

Have a great Mother's Day gift idea you want to share with Yours Truly readers? Send me a postcard with a brief—30 words or less—idea, include your first name, city and state, and you just might see it printed on a special page in next May's Yours Truly books.

I know next May is far off, but next month you'll find two new Yours Truly titles by Carolyn Zane and Carla Neggers—two more novels about unexpectedly meeting, dating and marrying Mr. Right.

Yours truly,

*Melissa Senate*

Editor

---

Please address questions and book requests to:
Silhouette Reader Service
U.S.: 3010 Walden Ave., P.O. Box 1325, Buffalo, NY 14269
Canadian: P.O. Box 609, Fort Erie, Ont. L2A 5X3

# MARIE FERRARELLA

*Let's Get Mommy Married*

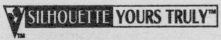

Published by Silhouette Books

America's Publisher of Contemporary Romance

SILHOUETTE BOOKS

ISBN 0-373-52019-0

LET'S GET MOMMY MARRIED

## About the author

**MARIE FERRARELLA:** I've been writing, simply and otherwise, since I was eleven. But mentally, I've been spinning stories since I was old enough to string two sentences together. Television was a huge influence. For instance, did you know that the Cartwright boys of "Bonanza" had a sister? (That's okay, they didn't know it, either.) Her name was Kit. Marty of "Spin and Marty" also had a sister (I can't remember her name, so I guess she wasn't very impressive.) Zorro had one, too (Zora—I was very young at the time and not overly creative). In each case, the heroine was feisty, brave and wonderful, and yes, she was me. Writing myself into the stories always made them that much more exciting for me.

I never lost that time-worn tradition. A piece of me, of my heart, is in each heroine, each story I write. That's why they're always so special to me. So here I go again, offering you my heart wrapped up in a story of love lost and then found. I hope it succeeds in giving you a little pleasure.

To Melissa Senate,
for input
and inspiration
Thank You

# 1

---

Dear K-LAS, I would like to win a date for my mom on Mother's Day because she hasn't had one in a long time. It's not because she's not pretty because she is. Real pretty. But she's very busy, working very hard so that I can have everything I want. But I want her to have something for *her*. Somebody to talk to when I'm not around. I'm not going to be a kid forever and Mom needs somebody to look out for her. But don't tell her I said so. She's thirty but looks a lot younger and she's got a real nice laugh. She likes old songs, old movies and to walk in the rain. Please make the guy handsome and tall, and if he plays baseball, that would be neat, too. But he's gotta be nice to my mom because she's the best.

Your friend,
Tommy Smith

P.S. Please send your letter to me instead of my mom because it's a surprise. Thank you.

A smile curved Rosemary Gallagher's mouth as she looked at the wide, childish scrawl on the page. Touched, she placed the letter on top of the small pile of potential winners that was forming on her desk.

What a neat kid, she thought. Who said motherhood was unrewarding? This Tommy Smith sounded every bit as precious, as wonderful, as her Danny.

Rosemary pushed her light brown bangs out of her eyes with the back of her hand. She was going to have to remember to trim them later. There were more important things on her mind at the moment. Unless there were some really outstanding letters coming in, Tommy's mother was going to be one of the ten winners in the contest she was running.

She'd sorted through the deluge of letters that had been forwarded to her from the radio station and winnowed them down to approximately twenty-five. Out of those, she was going to select ten single mothers. Ten women who would win a date for Mother's Day.

Once contacted, the women would have to fill out the forms she had spent weeks designing when she started her business. Forms that should, as accurately as possible, match them to their soulmates.

Soulmates, Inc., was the name of the personal dating service that she had established after cutbacks at the university had turned her from a full-time instructor on her way up to a part-time adjunct lecturer in need of a decent salary supplement. Soulmates, Inc., had been born on her kitchen counter, parented in equal parts by inspiration and desperation. After four years of hard work, it was now a thriving business that kept her more than sufficiently busy. So busy that two months ago she had invited her cousin Teri to work part-time for her.

Rosemary leaned back in her chair and stretched her hands over her head. The motion failed to alleviate the crick in her neck. She knew why she was tense. There was a deadline breathing down her neck. She had to choose the winners, contact them, process their forms and match them with suitable candidates—all in less than two weeks if she was to successfully pull off the publicity campaign she had engineered.

She wished Teri would get here. Even though her cousin worked only part-time, Rosemary sorely missed the extra help she provided. That and her endless chatter. Running on approximately four hours' sleep, she felt she needed someone around to help keep her from nodding off at her desk.

Rosemary reached for the file she normally kept next to her chair. Her outstretched fingers came in contact with air. She'd forgotten. Everything chewable had to be taken off the floor; otherwise it was quickly turned into shredded wheat via very intent puppy teeth.

With a long sigh, she rose and crossed to the file cabinet closest to her. There were two in the kitchen, aligned beside the pantry. The piles on top of them were growing larger and larger, threatening to come tumbling down. She was just going to have to find time to get to that, she thought. She had a new computer system and needed to key in everything to streamline her operations. Why was everything designed to make things simple always so complicated?

She heard a yip coming from the backyard. It reminded her why she'd only had four hours of sleep. As if she didn't have enough to do.

God, she must have been crazy to agree to allow a dog in the house. An untrained, unhousebroken dog. It was hard enough being a single mother of a small boy without being the single mother of a small boy with a dog.

Rosemary sighed again as she looked out the kitchen window into the backyard. There was her son, manfully trying to train a very inattentive dog. He had brought the dog—a strange mixture of shag, ears and a tail—home a week ago. He'd carried it in his arms, spouting the classic line, "Look what followed me home, Mom. Can I keep him?"

Rosemary's immediate reaction had been to give him a very firm no. The only dog she'd ever had as a child had been stuffed and sat in the middle of her bed. It never messed, threw up or ate her bedspread.

Danny's newfound dog had managed all of the above within the first few hours, but Danny's big blue eyes had melted her resistance.

She eyed the doggie spot cleaner that stood at the ready on her counter. It was almost half-gone. If it were up to her, the dog would be gone, as well. But she couldn't find it in her heart to deny her son anything that was within her power to grant. It wasn't easy for a boy growing up without a father.

It wasn't exactly a piece of cake for a wife without a husband, either, she thought ruefully. But she and Danny managed.

Just like the women in these letters seemed to manage. Rosemary smiled at the growing pile on her desk. Having Danny was an immense comfort. Even if he did bring in a stray mutt to add to the pandemonium that she whimsically called her life. She wouldn't have traded him for anything in the world.

He added that extra something to her days. He had even inspired her to hold this contest. "Win A Date For Mom on Mother's Day" had been her brainchild, but it was born out of something that Danny had said to her. He had wanted to give her "a real neat present" this year for Mother's Day because she'd allowed him to keep the dog.

Frazzled as she cleaned yet another accident from the living room rug, she'd looked up at her pride and joy. "Like what?"

He had thought for a long moment, hugging the puppy to him. The dog had licked his face with the enthusiasm only very young puppies had. Danny's face had lit up. "How about a date?"

Rising to her feet, Rosemary could only laugh at the suggestion. It seemed an ironic thing to say, considering that she conducted a personal dating service out of her home.

But then it occurred to her that there might be more little boys out there who felt the way Danny did. They wanted to do something special for their mothers, but had no money to buy anything. A date would be a very special gift. And free. The more she'd thought about it, the more she'd liked the idea.

The publicity she'd gotten from the radio ad had increased business for Soulmates, Inc. It helped make up for the fact that she now owned a very chewed-up pair of dark brown suede boots.

The sliding-glass door squeaked as Danny pushed it open with his elbow. His arms were filled with dog. "So, how's it going?"

"Okay." The dog, dubbed Rocky by her son despite the fact that they had discovered it was a female, was all paws and wiggles, desperate to get out of the half nelson Danny had on her. Those nails needed clipping, Rosemary thought. "I could ask you the same thing. Getting her to mind any better?"

Rosemary knew the answer to that one, but thought it might make Danny feel better if she pretended to believe that he was succeeding. Danny had always loved animals, but it was one thing to pass them on the street or to watch them on educational television specials, and it was quite another having an animal in your own home, one that made confetti out of shoe boxes—with the shoes still in them.

"Yeah." The answer was far too enthusiastic to be genuine. He announced it quickly, breathlessly, the way someone did when he wanted to get past a lie.

*Poor Danny.* Rosemary beckoned him closer. Face level to the dog, Rosemary pulled back a little and then scratched Rocky behind the ears.

She smiled at Danny. Hope mingled with frustration in his blue eyes. "It takes time, honey."

It seemed as if the tail was wagging the dog. A vibration undulated all the way up the length of the puppy. The next moment evidence of the dog's joy rained down on her kitchen floor. Rosemary looked down, resigned. At least it wasn't newly polished.

"Take her out back, Danny. She obviously isn't running on empty."

He nodded. Dog still in hand, he retraced his steps through the kitchen to the sliding back door. Rosemary rose and took hold of the mop, which she no longer bothered putting away. With luck, if she kept at it, the house wouldn't smell like a barn before the dog was housebroken.

Danny was still in the kitchen, one hand on the door, the other wrapped firmly around the squirming dog. "You didn't tell me. How is it going?"

Rosemary wasn't sure what he was getting at.

"The contest, I mean."

The spot was erased. Rosemary rinsed out the mop and then leaned the handle against the counter. No doubt it would be pressed into service soon enough. She glanced at her son as she wiped her hands. "You seem awfully interested in my work all of a sudden."

Danny looked affronted, as if he'd been interested in his mother's work all along. "Well, gee, you're using my idea."

She smiled as she sat down at the desk again. "And a very good one it was, too."

Rosemary looked at the stacks of mail on the counter. They vied for space with the built-in burners. She moved them to a safer place. Clutter was closing in on her. Right after Mother's Day, she was going to take a couple of days off and really clean.

"Because of you, we're getting a great deal of publicity for the service." Which was true. In the three days that the ad had run on Chris Maverick's five-to-nine slot on K-LAS, daily mail seemed to have tripled.

Like a miniature CEO dabbling in his company's operations, Danny methodically surveyed the incoming mail, his eyes sweeping along the sorted piles on his mother's desk.

"So, did you pick them yet? The winners?" he elaborated before she could answer.

She slid open a letter with the ivory letter opener that Patrick had given her for their last Valentine's Day. Her hand curved around the carved handle lovingly. "I'm working on it."

Danny edged closer with the dog. Rocky began whimpering, obviously in protest at being kept dangling. Her hind legs hung down almost the length of Danny's body. "Can I see which ones you picked so far?"

Danny had always referred to what she did as "that mushy-making stuff." Was her little guy growing up that fast? She placed the letter opener on the desk and studied his intent face. It looked like a miniature of her own, except with blond hair. That had come from Patrick. "You *are* interested in this, aren't you?"

His shoulders lifted and fell beneath the striped T-shirt. "Sure." He shifted the dog to keep her from falling. "Maybe I'll help you pick them."

He sounded downright eager. He *was* growing up. "I'll run them past you later," she promised solemnly. Rosemary waved a finger at Rocky. "Right now, you've got a little lady on your hands who *really* wants to christen something else. Out." Rosemary pointed toward the door leading into the backyard.

Struggling, Danny slid the door all the way open and then shut it again. Rosemary watched as the puppy finally leapt out of his arms and made a break for freedom. Thank goodness she'd never gotten around to planting flower beds. They'd probably all be dug up by now.

Rosemary forced her mind back on her work. It tickled her that Danny was taking such an interest in the contest. Maybe she would get his input, just to make him feel more important. His self-esteem was very much intact, but it didn't hurt to bolster it from time to time. At eleven, Danny was the man of the family, as he had been for the past nine years.

Her little man, she mused. Except that he wasn't so little anymore. He was going through a growth spurt and it wouldn't be all that long before he would be taller than she was, out on his own, getting serious about a girlfriend and—

Rosemary stopped abruptly and laughed at herself. Here she was, marrying him off, and he hadn't graduated elementary school yet. It was just that the days seemed to trickle by one by one and somehow the years just zipped along.

Her eyes narrowed as she looked at the floor near the counter.

*Speaking of trickle,* she thought, she'd missed a spot. With a sigh, Rosemary rose and reached for the mop again.

She'd just rinsed the mop out when she heard the doorbell. At this rate the contest winners would be chosen by *next* Mother's Day. Rosemary checked her watch and realized that it was probably Teri, running late as usual. Teri, eight months her junior, had been born three days late. In thirty years, she hadn't been able to kick the habit.

Harried, looking as if the wind had seen fit to blow her in, Teri entered with a mail sack that looked as if it was more than half-filled.

"Hi, I stopped by the post office to collect our mail." Teri made her way into the kitchen and dropped the sack on the floor. "This contest is a hoot. I never realized how many single people there were out there, looking for someone to love."

Rosemary prudently picked up the sack and placed it on an empty stool. She grinned. "It's what keeps us in business, Teri."

Teri, as blond as Rosemary was dark, noted the strategic replacement of the sack. "White Fang still chewing everything in sight?"

Rosemary waved a hand. "Don't get me started. I don't know why I agreed to this."

Teri laughed as she opened the refrigerator and helped herself to a can of soda. "I do. Because you're a pushover. But that's okay, you're a lovable one." She took a quick pull from the can and then used it as an extension of her hand. She waved at the neat stacks of paper on Rosemary's desk. The woman could make order out of a hurricane, she thought. "How's Danny's brainstorm coming along?"

Rosemary nodded as she scanned the letter she had just opened. Too well worded. This one wasn't written by any under-twelve-year-old she was acquainted with. This was definitely done by an adult attempting to sound like a child. The simple words were misspelled and the difficult ones, the ones a child wouldn't use, were all spelled correctly.

She placed the letter on the pile on the far side of her desk. These would be rejected gently and mailed back with a Soulmates form in hopes that whoever did write them would avail themselves of her services honestly.

"It's kind of hard to choose, but I'm getting there." She looked at the sack. "Since you picked those up at our regular P.O. box, I'm assuming that they have nothing to do with the contest.''

Teri shook her head. "Not unless some short person got enterprising on us. These are probably all from people who heard about the dating service on the radio.'' Teri grinned, taking her time as she sauntered to the table. "That was a nice touch." She sighed, a dreamy smile on her lips. "You know, that guy who did the announcement has the sexiest voice I've ever heard. Like warm rainwater sliding along your face in the fall.''

*And wouldn't he like to hear that!* Rosemary thought, amused at the description, although, now that she turned it over in her mind, it was rather apt. Chris Maverick did have a sexy voice. It was his trademark.

"His other parts aren't too shabby, either," she added as she began opening another letter.

Interest immediately registered in Teri's clear blue eyes. Her soda can abruptly met the countertop as she abandoned it.

"Oh?" She moved closer to Rosemary, peering at her face. Her cousin was holding out on her. Hallelujah! "And just what parts have you seen?"

Rosemary could tell by her expression that Teri's imagination was off at a full gallop. "He's my neighbor, Teri. I've seen him working in the yard.''

Teri's mouth dropped open as she simultaneously sank into the chair next to Rosemary's, her knees collapsing. Rosemary had mentioned her neighbors only a couple of times. Chris was Chris Maverick. She'd never made the connection before.

"Chris Maverick is your neighbor?"

Teri said it as if she'd just announced that she was having an affair with Mel Gibson.

"Yes," Rosemary said patiently, as if addressing a dim-witted child. "That's how I got the idea to have the contest on the radio." It had happened quite by accident, really, but she wasn't going to go into that now. The upshot of it was that Chris had volunteered to help. He was really very nice, if somewhat too good-looking for her to feel completely comfortable around him. "He managed to get me a lower advertising rate."

The look on Teri's face was nothing short of wolfish. "Is that before or after you saw his other non-shabby parts?"

Teri clearly wasn't going to give it up until she explained this and debunked her cousin's obvious fantasy. "The nonshabby parts I was referring to were completely clothed, Teri. Get your mind above street level. The man just wears his jeans rather well, that's all." Rosemary frowned. They had to get to work. She hated falling behind. "I told you all this at least once."

If she did, Teri didn't recall it. She was positive she would have remembered being told that Chris Maverick was living a few feet away from her cousin.

"Probably when one of the twins was screaming in my ear. You know that mothers of twins need everything repeated at least twice." She settled back and opened a letter, though her mind and her eyes were not on her work. "So, tell me more about this nonshabby person."

Rosemary looked at her cousin. She recognized that glint in Teri's eye. It had matchmaker written all over it. She might be the one who ultimately made matches for other people, but it was Teri who was always on *her* case, urging that she take advantage of her own growing stable of male applicants.

Rosemary looked away as she picked up another piece of mail. She didn't have time for this. "Get that look out of your eyes, Teri."

Teri fiddled with a letter. She loved Rosemary far more than she could have loved a sister. They had shared everything together, from a consuming crush on Shaun Cassidy in "The Hardy Boys," to agonizing all-nighters in college, to the joys of weddings, childbirth and the tragedy of Patrick's untimely death.

"You know, Rosie, I never figured out how you could have a dating service and never go out on a date yourself." Teri barely glanced at the letter in her hand. "Ever hear of 'physician, heal thyself'?"

Rosemary reached over and took the letter out of Teri's hand. "Yes, but I've never heard of a physician taking out his own appendix." The form was one of their preprinted ones. She glanced at the name and placed it in the male pile.

Teri shook her head. Rosemary was going to have to have a change of heart, and soon. "You make it sound as if dating's painful."

That was the word for it, Rosemary thought. Painful. Just the very thought of going out on a date, of making coherent conversation, made shivers run down her spine, and they were not of the pleasant variety. She shrugged carelessly. "It is, for some of us."

It seemed to Teri that Rosemary was refuting everything that the dating service was supposed to stand for. "But Rosie, you were married—"

It was a familiar road and she had driven down it with Teri before. "And I loved it. I think everyone should be as happy as I was with Patrick—"

Teri felt exasperation bubbling just beneath the surface. Damn, but Rosemary didn't make sense sometimes. If *she* found herself single again and sitting in the middle of this dating service, she'd feel as if she had struck gold.

"So...?"

Rosemary wasn't going to allow herself to be sucked into another pointless discussion. "So I have this service, matching the right people together and sending them off to a hopefully happy ending." It was one thing to think of others dating. It was entirely another to imagine herself in that situation.

Maybe she was just being dense, Teri thought, but she didn't understand. "And none of these male applicants—" she waved her hand at the file cabinet that contained copies of forms sent in by eligible bachelors "—have ever struck you as interesting, as worth the trouble of putting on panty hose and high heels?"

Rosemary purposely wiggled her bare toes within the sandals she wore. Sandals that the dog found particularly tempting.

"Maybe, but that doesn't mean I want to go through the dating ritual." She saw the frown on Teri's face. "I think hang gliding is interesting, but I'm not about to strap on wings and jump off a cliff." Maybe she was just a coward. Maybe Patrick's memory got in the way. She leaned forward, wishing Teri could understand and stop playing that one, tedious note. "Something happens when I go out on a date. I feel this pressure to be witty, funny, entertaining—"

Teri didn't see the problem. "You *are* all those things."

"Maybe, but not on call." She'd gone out exactly twice since Patrick died. And both dates had ended up as miserable failures. "The woman they ask out is not the woman they get on a date. Something falls apart inside." Rosemary shivered just at the memory. "I freeze up, like an actor with stage fright." That was it, she realized. That was the best way to explain what she felt to Teri. "I get stage fright on dates." She waved a dismissive hand. "And it's not worth it to me. I'm perfectly happy with my life just the way it is—"

Rosemary heard a howl and automatically winced. "Except for the dog, of course, but hopefully, that'll change."

Teri sighed, momentarily surrendering. "Have it your way." She sifted through the pile of letters closest to her. She stopped when she saw the letter that

Rosemary had been reading just before she'd arrived. "Hey, I like this one."

Rosemary glanced up and saw which one Teri was referring to. She nodded. "Cute, isn't it? It's in the finals."

Teri replaced it on top of the pile. "Well, it gets my vote."

She loved her cousin dearly, but Teri had a slap-dash method that sometimes got under her skin. Rosemary straightened the pile. "You haven't read the others yet."

Teri reached behind her and wrapped her fingers around the can of soda, bringing it to her mouth. "I will, but this one does sound sweet."

"I know." There was no arguing with that. "It makes me think of something that Danny would write." She glanced at the letter again. "Except that the spelling is a lot better."

"Mom, she got through the fence!" Danny's cry was like a call to arms.

Rosemary exchanged looks with Teri. "Yes, Virginia, there is a Santa Claus. Maybe she's trying to run away."

Danny rushed into the kitchen. "Rocky went through the neighbor's fence. You know that hole?"

Rosemary closed her eyes. There were two holes in the fence that framed the backyard, one on either side. "Oh, great. That means she's either in the O'Donnells' snapping turtle pond, or I'm repaying Chris

Maverick's generosity by having my son's dog baptize his begonias.''

Opening her eyes, she fixed her son with a weary look. "Which neighbor, Danny?"

Danny shifted from foot to foot, eager to be off in pursuit. "That guy's. Mr. Maverick."

"Terrific." Pushing back her chair, she rose. "This may take a while, Teri."

Teri cocked her head, amused. Her eyes were dancing. "Do I get to meet Mr. Nonshabby Parts?"

Rosemary shook her head as she walked out of the kitchen. Teri was hopeless. "You're married," she tossed over her shoulder.

"But I'm not dead," Teri called after her, then laughed as she sat back at the desk.

Danny looked over his shoulder at Teri and grinned broadly. She winked back, then got down to work.

This was not turning out to be one of Rosemary's better days. She marched up to Chris Maverick's front door and rang the doorbell. She absolutely hated bothering people. But she supposed that it was already past that point now. Her son's dog was making herself at home in the man's yard and causing who knew what kind of damage.

The door opened on the second ring. Christopher Maverick was standing in the doorway, all six foot two of him, barefoot, dripping, with a towel slung around his bare shoulders and a black towel wrapped around his taut, flat stomach.

Dear God, she could iron shirts on that stomach, Rosemary thought before she realized that she was staring. Chagrined, she raised her eyes to his face.

It was difficult forming words when she felt as if she'd swallowed her tongue. Rosemary tried anyway. Her words came out in a rush that she thought was positively adolescent.

"I'm sorry, I didn't mean to drag you out of the shower, but my son's dog is in your yard."

If he was annoyed, Chris didn't show it. Instead his expression was completely affable. "I thought I heard yelping."

He brushed one end of the towel he had around his neck over his hair, drying it. Several droplets of water rained down. Chris stepped back and gestured for her and Danny to enter the house. "Let's go get her."

He led the way to the rear of the house. Rosemary felt something akin to Jell-O forming in her stomach and oozing down through her knees. It wasn't as if she hadn't seen an almost-naked man before—just not in the past nine years.

Somehow she managed to find her tongue again. "We don't mean to be any trouble. Why don't you just go back upstairs and get dressed? Danny and I can take it from here."

Chris looked at her over a very broad, bare shoulder. "No trouble," he assured her as he strode ahead of her.

*Oh, yes,* she thought. *Trouble. Very definite trouble.* The man had no hips. How the hell did that towel stay on?

Chris pulled up on the lock and opened the sliding back door. The next moment Rocky came bolting into the house, her paws freshly encrusted in mud. Within a heartbeat, there were muddy tracks everywhere.

This was getting to be a nightmare. "Oh, God, I'm so sorry." Rosemary made a lunge for the dog but the animal was faster than she was. "I can come back and clean all this up."

Chris shook his head. "Don't worry about it—I have a maid service that comes in twice a month. And there's nothing to be sorry about. He's just a puppy." Miraculously, as if attracted to the low, sensual tones, Rocky ceased fleeing and presented herself at Chris's feet as if she were his dog. Laughing, he bent and scratched the dog behind the ears.

"She," Danny corrected. Seeing his chance, he scooped up the dog.

"She?" Chris raised a brow. "I thought I heard you calling out 'Rocky' yesterday."

"I did." Danny grinned broadly. "Her name's Rocky. After the Colorado Rockies." To his delight, Danny saw that the choice seemed to make perfect sense to Chris.

Bored with tranquillity, Rocky was already wiggling out of Danny's grasp. Jumping, she sank her teeth into Chris's towel and then landed on the floor with a thud.

Rosemary gasped and swung around just as Rocky went galloping across the room, the towel firmly gripped in her young jaws, waving behind her like a trophy of her latest adventure.

"Oh, God, I'm sorry." She kept saying that, Rosemary thought impotently. She stood with her back to Chris, facing the front door. "Danny, get Rocky," she ordered.

Rosemary felt herself turning crimson. She'd swung around, but not before she had seen far more of Chris Maverick's nonshabby parts than she figured he wanted her to see.

Chris took the towel he had slung over his shoulders and did some quick rearranging. "No problem," he said in that same calm, steady voice. "I used to have a dog myself. Every boy needs a dog, right, Danny?"

"Right."

His eyes were full of amusement as he moved into Rosemary's line of vision. "But I think I will go upstairs and get dressed now. You can see yourselves out?"

The towel he had on now was little more than a long hand towel. Rosemary felt her mouth growing dry as cotton. "Absolutely," she murmured.

Coming to, she scooted Danny toward the door. She didn't quite remember the walk home.

# 2

Teri took off her glasses as Rosemary entered the kitchen. Danny was directly behind her, doing a balancing act with the dog in his arms. The dog made it clear that she would have rather had the use of her feet, but Danny looked determined to carry her. Grinning broadly, he presented his pride and joy to Teri.

Teri leaned forward to scratch the dog behind her ears. "Ah, here's the missing member of the family now."

Rosemary groaned audibly as she sank down in her chair. "Please, don't remind me." She glanced accusingly at Rocky. Just how long did it take to housebreak a puppy, anyway?

Danny looked at his mother, crestfallen. "Don't you like Rocky, Mom?"

She remembered how important it had seemed to her at Danny's age to have her parents' approval. Rosemary mustered a smile. "Sure I do. I'd just like her a whole lot better if she were trained."

Teri made no effort to hide her smirk. "Oh, I don't know. I think she's pretty well-trained right now. She got you into Mr. Terrific's lair, didn't she?"

Danny looked from Teri to his mother. "Who's Mr. Terrific, Mom, and what's a lair?"

"Teri's talking about Mr. Maverick, honey. And she means his home. Teri's just having a little bit of difficulty expressing herself this afternoon." The warning look Rosemary aimed at Teri missed its mark entirely. Teri merely fluttered her lashes as she reached for her glasses.

"Oh, him. We got Chris, um, Mr. Maverick, out of the shower. He was wearing a towel and he was all wet," Danny said in a rush as he hurried to the back door.

He was beginning to distinguish between Rocky's different movements and this one had "elimination" written all over it. He didn't notice that Teri had dropped her glasses as well as her jaw.

"And he didn't even mind when Rocky ran off with his towel." Hurrying, Danny slid the screen door closed behind him.

If she wasn't already sitting, Teri knew that she would have collapsed into her chair. Her eyes were huge as she looked at Rosemary. "You saw him naked?"

It was something that she'd rather not talk about. Rosemary waved a dismissive hand at her cousin. If she let her, Teri would go on about this indefinitely and the whole afternoon would be shot.

"I turned my head."

This went beyond anything Teri could assimilate. She half rose in her seat. "You did *what?*"

Rosemary shrugged. "I saw Rocky make a lunge for the towel and I turned my head. End of story."

Teri shook her head in stunned disbelief. "You have got to be one of a kind, Rosie." She picked up her glasses, then looked at Rosemary. "The man was actually naked?"

A grin crept up to Rosemary's lips. "No, he still had a towel around his shoulders."

"Oh, God." Teri clamped a hand over her heart. "And you're standing here, talking to me? Rosie, are you getting slow-witted in your old age?"

Rosemary looked down her nose at Teri. "Might I remind you that my old age is your old age, dear cousin?"

"Only numerically." There were times Teri despaired over her cousin. This was a golden opportunity Rosemary had allowed to slide through her fingers. "Some people apparently are born old."

Sometimes the way Teri thought was a complete mystery to her. "What was I supposed to do, jump him?"

"No, get *acquainted.*" Teri stretched out the word. Rosemary raised a brow in her direction. Teri looked at her innocently. "Hey, I've seen pictures of that guy on the sides of buses. He's absolutely gorgeous."

The photos were all part of an ad campaign to get people to tune in to Chris's program, "Roamin' With

The Maverick." It was obviously working on the female population, Rosemary thought, if Teri was any barometer.

"Yes," she agreed patiently, "he is gorgeous—"

"So?" If eagerness had a name, Rosemary thought, it was Teri.

Just what was it Teri had expected her to do? "So, I have work to do." Sighing inwardly, she reached for another stack of envelopes.

Teri felt like shaking Rosemary. "Danny's in the backyard with White Fang, and the man may still not have dried off yet. What are you doing here?"

"Working." Doggedly, Rosemary tried to do just that. What had gotten into Teri today, anyway? She was always pushy, but this was a new high even for her.

Teri opened her mouth with a retort, then shut it again. There was no arguing with Rosemary when she had that look on her face. Back to Plan A.

With the tip of her finger, Teri pushed toward her the last letter Rosemary had selected before she had run off to retrieve the dog. "I reread this one while you were ignoring opportunities, and it is definitely a winner."

Rosemary nodded. Danny let himself back into the kitchen. The dog was trotting behind him, looking as docile as if she was a pull toy.

Yeah, right, Rosemary thought. And how long would that last?

She looked toward Teri. "Well, we're agreed so far." Rosemary indicated the smaller pile of contest letters. "Only four more to find."

Deciding to tackle that next, she reached for another letter. Teri beat her to it, snatching it almost out of her grasp. Rosemary looked at her quizzically.

Teri pulled the other letters toward her. "Why don't I go through the rest of these and you start sending out the forms on the ones you've chosen so far?"

This was a switch. Teri never took the initiative. Maybe the vicarious impression of a naked, dripping Chris Maverick had had a positive effect. "You certainly seem eager to get this contest moving."

The smile on Teri's lips was just a bit too wide, even for Teri. It made Rosemary wonder what was up. "Call it the romantic in me."

Rosemary laughed. "I'm not quite sure I'd call it that—"

The simultaneous yelp and ringing doorbell abruptly cut Rosemary's statement short. She rose and crossed to the front door, hoping that the yelp didn't translate into another large stain on the carpet somewhere in the house. Even though the carpet cleaner was doing a great job in erasing the telltale marks, Rosemary felt as if it was just a matter of time before the entire carpet became saturated.

She unlocked the door. *Now what?*

A drier, clothed Chris Maverick was standing in her doorway. He was wearing a white V-neck sweater with the sleeves pushed up along his forearms and a pair of jeans that looked as if they had been spray painted onto his very muscular thighs. If she tried hard, she could swear she could hear Teri salivating from here.

There wasn't a trace of embarrassment about him. Maybe the man ran naked through his living room all the time. Well, Rosemary thought, she was embarrassed enough for both of them. She knew it was horribly unsophisticated of her, but the mere thought of Chris, detoweled, had a blush threatening to take over again. She could almost feel it forging a trail up her neck into her cheeks.

She was blushing, Chris realized, stunned and somehow touched at the same time. He didn't think women did that anymore. He'd certainly never seen it happen firsthand.

Chris studied her face and thought the added color was charming. Rosemary Gallagher herself was rather charming, in a soft, understated way. He'd seen her the first day he had moved in, over three months ago, and had immediately been attracted to her. The attraction had taken root when he had discovered through her son that she wasn't married.

But the lady had given off signals that she was not interested in anything other than being neighborly. She'd offered him cake, a cold drink and the use of her phone until his was hooked up. There were no other offers, implied or stated.

If he thought about it, Chris found that rather refreshing. In his line of work there were a great many groupies around, all of whom wanted to boast that they had spent the night with a radio personality. In their eagerness to catch a bit of stardust, they had elevated him to the level of a minor celebrity.

It was enough to turn a guy's head if he wasn't well grounded. It was also enough to sour a guy on the idea of ever finding a sweet, old-fashioned girl. One who liked him because he was a slightly imperfect, left-handed guy with a nice smile and a passion for old movies and old songs. Women like that just didn't exist.

Or did they? he wondered, looking at her. "Hi."

It was perfectly stupid to feel embarrassed like this, Rosemary told herself. After all, it wasn't *her* fault that the dog had grabbed his towel. She certainly hadn't trained Rocky to do that. And he was the one who hadn't retreated when she'd suggested that he get dressed. God knows, he didn't look as if he was embarrassed by the incident.

Reasoning notwithstanding, Rosemary still couldn't keep the red stain from inching up along her neck. What was he doing here, anyway?

"Hi," she murmured in response.

Another yip, this time much more plaintive, floated through the air. Chris read the question in her eyes and nodded in the general direction of the obviously distressed puppy. "You seem to be having some trouble with your new friend."

Rosemary half turned her head, hoping that whatever it was could be cleaned up or straightened out. "Trouble doesn't begin to cover it."

She wasn't going to let him in, he thought, and wondered why. Most women would have had him in a compromising situation by now, especially after the towel incident. "I'm a fair hand at training dogs, if you'd like any help."

Rosemary was aware of Teri hovering beside her elbow like a heat-seeking missile trying to reach its target. Rosemary kept her hand firmly on the doorknob. "I'll keep that in mind, but I really don't want to impose."

There was another yelp and the crash of something heavy and probably expensive. Rosemary closed her eyes for a moment, gathering strength. When she opened them again, it was to look into Chris's very amused green eyes.

"Maybe I'd better impose."

"It's no imposition at all. I'm volunteering."

Rosemary moved aside as she opened the door for him. She managed to successfully block the image of his bare body from her mind. After all, if he could live with her having seen him, she could live with having seen him.

Ah, but the trick was to do it without feeling her pulse rush, she thought.

She gestured toward the family room, where the noises were coming from. "Anything you can do with her will be greatly appreciated."

Chris's soft, liquid green eyes washed over her and he smiled. Very slowly. The smile bloomed like a flower unfurling its petals up to the early morning sun.

Rosemary felt something within her responding. Brightening. But since it had absolutely nowhere to go from there, she banked it.

Chris looked around. The house was a mirror image of his own. And yet there were soft, feminine touches everywhere, clearly giving it an individual look. The similarities yet differences made him smile even more. He arched a brow.

"Where?"

She gestured toward the rear of the house, where the family room was located. "Just follow the yipping—" Rosemary glanced at Teri. "Ignoring my cousin as you go, of course."

Feeling she had been far too patient as it was, Teri moved forward, her hand extended toward Chris. "Hi, I'm Teri Lawson. I help Rosemary out with Soulmates, Inc. And I think you should sue the bus line."

He'd heard a great many opening lines, but that one was a first for him. Suppressing a laugh, Chris shook his head as if to clear it. "Excuse me?"

"The picture that they have of you," Teri explained. As usual, her brain was way ahead of her tongue. "It doesn't begin to do you justice."

Chris laughed. "Thanks." He went to find Danny and the dog.

"'Sue the bus line,'" Rosemary repeated incredulously as she walked back to the kitchen. "Why didn't you just lick his shoes?"

The criticism left Teri completely unfazed. The man *was* better-looking in person than he was on the Number 65 crosstown. God, if only she were single again...

"I figure the dog'll take care of that part of him." Teri craned her neck, watching Chris disappear into the family room. "You're living next door to that?"

"We've already established that fact." Rosemary tried to keep her voice nonchalant. It wasn't as if she hadn't noticed how handsome Chris was—she had. Very definitely. But she had also been serious when she'd told Teri how she felt about dating. That was for other people and she certainly encouraged it, but when it came to doing it herself, she would rather just daydream.

In daydreams she always said the right things, had the right comebacks, made her date laugh instead of feel painfully embarrassed for her. When she had gone out on those dates she'd mentioned, she had felt like an accident waiting to happen. A deadly dull accident.

Teri sat down opposite her, but if her mind hadn't been on her work before, it definitely wasn't on it now. "Talk about wasting your opportunities. Rosie, if it were me—"

Rosemary was tired of going around this. She had her stand and she was sticking with it. "Well, it's *not* you, it's me, and you know I hate being called Rosie."

They had called her Rosie as a child not because it was short for Rosemary but because she always had such an optimistic view of the future. Right now, it annoyed her a great deal.

Teri leaned back on her chair and rocked slightly, her eyes on her cousin. "As I recall, you hate being called stupid, too."

"Teri, if I have to explain things to you one more time, I'm having the whole thing recorded."

Teri raised her hands in temporary surrender. Rosemary's time would come, and a lot sooner than her cousin anticipated if she had anything to say about it.

"I know, I know, the shoemaker's kids go barefoot and the matchmaker goes celibate." Teri picked up a letter then tossed it down again, frowning. "It's just that I hate to see such a waste." She glanced toward the family room. "At least look in on the guy and see how it's going."

That was something she was *not* about to do. "People don't like being watched," Rosemary insisted.

She wasn't going to push, Teri reminded herself, she had promised herself that she wasn't going to push. After all, things were going to work themselves out.

She couldn't help herself. "He's a radio personality, Rosemary. Being watched goes with the territory."

"Radio," Rosemary repeated without bothering to look up. "Not television."

Teri tried again. "What's the harm? Besides, you *must* know him in some capacity if you asked him to advertise the contest."

That had taken a great deal of courage. Considered friendly, outgoing and gregarious, Rosemary still really hated to impose. "That was business," she explained.

"So?" Teri raised her shoulders until they almost touched her earlobes. "Mean business."

Rosemary smiled and shook her head as she looked up at her cousin. Teri worried about her, she knew that. And in her own dogged way, Teri meant well. Even if she had trouble taking no for an answer. "Teri, I've had my romance, I've had my marriage."

Teri leaned forward, whispering into Rosemary's ear. "It's like kidneys. You're allowed to have two."

"Yes," Rosemary agreed whimsically. "But you can make do on one."

Teri knew defeat when it stared her in the face. "Are you sure we're related?"

Rosemary laughed. Maybe now they could get some work accomplished. She brushed her hair out of her eyes. "So Mother says."

She had managed to read down to the second paragraph of a letter when Chris interrupted. Knocking on the doorjamb, he stuck his head in the doorway. "Excuse me, do you have any treats?"

Rosemary felt as if her pulse had jumped a full inch in her wrist. "Well, there's chocolate cake in the refriger—"

He laughed, shaking his head. Rosemary felt disarmed and addled at the same time. "No, I meant for the dog. It makes training easier."

He was actually serious about this. She had half expected him to leave in exasperation after five minutes with the dog. Any sane person would have. Rocky had a tendency to bounce off all four walls, leaving little calling cards as she went.

"Oh." Rosemary rose to her feet, smoothing down the edge of her blouse. "Dog treats. I knew that. Sure." She beckoned him to follow her to the pantry. "Right in here." There was a box of treats right next to the oatmeal. She offered the whole thing to him but he took out only three. "Bribing her?"

He slipped the three treats, shaped like little colored dog bones, into the pocket of his jeans. She wondered if they were going to be smashed there into a million pieces. How did he managed to get his hand into his pocket in the first place? There didn't seem to be space enough for a prayer, much less a hand.

"Sure. Everyone works a lot better if there's a reward waiting at the end." He noticed that Rosemary wasn't following him to the family room. He raised a brow. "Would you like to watch?"

She was tempted, but she wasn't the type to play hooky and there was all this work to do. "I—"

Teri was behind her, all but shoving her toward the family room, or, more accurately, into Chris's arms. "She'd like to watch," she assured Chris. "Watch," she ordered Rosemary. "I haven't been in for two days. I can certainly pick up a little of the slack. You deserve to take it easy for a while."

This was going too far, even for Teri, Rosemary thought. She'd all but tagged her ear and handed her to Chris.

"She works too hard," Teri told Chris solemnly as she shooed Rosemary away.

Rosemary didn't care to be discussed as if she was in another room. "In this business, you have to," Rosemary said defensively. "You never know when a dry period is going to hit."

If the work was there, she intended to take advantage of it, not wander off to watch a dog being trained. Even if the trainer was someone who could melt kneecaps at thirty paces.

Chris nodded knowingly. "Tell me about it. It's the same with being a radio announcer. One day you're working, opening fan mail, the next day, there's a pink slip in your paycheck."

He was pulling their leg, Teri thought. Who in their right minds would fire a disc jockey whose voice could melt frozen butter?

"That hasn't happened to you," Teri scoffed in disbelief.

He smiled at the compliment. "More than once."

"No." Teri's mouth formed a perfect circle.

Rosemary could feel her agitation, as well as her mortification, growing at a breathtaking rate. Any second now Teri was going to offer her to Chris on a silver platter. She could just see her doing it, gushing something like, "You two have so much in common." It was time to get Chris away from here.

"You're right," she said quickly. "I should watch you train Rocky. That way I can help Danny. And if you could possibly recommend a way I could get her to stop that awful whining and sleep through the night, I'd be permanently in your debt."

"All puppies whine," Chris told her. He stopped just short of the family room and looked at Rosemary in mild surprise. "You haven't been going to her when she whines, have you?"

His tone indicated that she had done something dumb. She was tempted to deny it, but she had to be honest. Rosemary nodded.

Rather than a lecture or a high-handed smirk, he smiled at her. "You really are soft-hearted, aren't you?"

Rosemary shrugged. "I thought that she had to go..." Her voice trailed off. "You know."

Yes, he knew, and he thought it rather cute that she couldn't bring herself to say it. Some of the women he'd met turned the air blue within five minutes.

"They learn to hold it," he assured her. "You don't want her getting the upper hand, do you?"

The way Rosemary saw it, Rocky already had. "Not particularly." She looked into the family room and saw Danny on the floor, with the puppy nipping at his shoes, his shirt and all parts in-between. He was giggling. Rosemary's heart warmed. "But I thought it was kind of cruel to leave her locked up all night."

Chris shook his head. "She'll never learn to sleep straight through if you go to her every time she cries." He saw the way Rosemary was looking at her son. "Did you do that with Danny when he was a baby?"

Each and every time. She'd stumbled into his room, instinct rather than vision guiding her steps. "Guilty as charged."

She really was rather unique, he thought. Chris shook his head with a laugh. "Well, he seems to have turned out just fine, but I don't recommend doing that with your dog."

Placing his hand at the small of her back, Chris guided Rosemary into the family room. Rosemary glanced over her shoulder and saw that Teri was still watching them. There was a very pleased look on her face. Rosemary mouthed, "Shut up."

Teri had the good grace to stop smiling and lower her eyes back to her work. But Rosemary could have sworn that even at this distance she detected traces of the smirk on Teri's lips.

Unlike her, Teri saw a match everywhere. Teri just didn't understand that some people preferred not to be attached. Or rather, preferred not to go through the agony of finding their way through the brambles to *become* attached.

Chris took his position in front of the dog. Rocky waved her tail madly. He probably saw a great deal of that, Rosemary thought.

"Now, you've got to show the puppy's who's boss. Dogs are pack animals, and you and Danny have to be the lead dogs."

Rosemary frowned. Now she had to become a dog? The whole idea was to have the dog become more civilized, not them more animal-like.

"The only dogs I ever came in contact with were Lassie and Rin Tin Tin in the movies. They were toilet trained, didn't smell and knew not to chew the fringes off my shawl." She thought of the unraveled heap she had discovered in her bedroom this morning and jerked a thumb at Rocky. "This one obviously hasn't read her Lassie manual."

Chris laughed. "No, maybe not, but she can be trained."

Danny looked up at him, confused. "To read the manual?"

Chris shook his head. "No, to rescue Timmy from the well."

Rosemary didn't want a rescue dog or one that did long division. She just wanted a house dog that didn't bring down the house five minutes after entry. "I'd settle for not making small rivers in my living room."

That was his first order of business. "Easy enough." He addressed his instructions to Danny. "Every time she squats, pick her up, say 'No' sharply, and take her outside. Once she does what you want her to, say 'Good dog.' After a while, it sinks in. It's basically like toilet training a baby, only easier."

Rosemary laughed. He made it sound too simple. "My baby didn't make a deposit on the hearth."

Danny looked at her aghast. "Mom!"

She flashed him a smile. "Sorry." Rosemary turned her attention to Chris. "How do you know so much about dogs?" She knew he didn't have one of his own. At some point or other in the past three months, she was sure she would have heard it.

He had a fond look in his eyes when he answered. She expected him to say that his last girlfriend had had one. "My parents own a kennel and they breed dogs."

Danny's eyes looked as if they were going to roll out of his head. "Really?"

Chris couldn't resist the temptation any longer. Reaching over, he ruffled Danny's hair. The boy reminded him of an eager, young puppy himself. A sheepdog. "Really." He looked at Rosemary. "Maybe you and your mother would like to visit it sometime?"

That was like asking Danny if he wanted a season's pass to Disneyland. "Could we, Mom? Could we?"

She assumed that the invitation was extended with the same conviction of "Let's do lunch." Rosemary gestured toward the dog. For form's sake only.

"Let's concentrate on this dog first." Danny still looked at her hopefully. "Besides, I've got a lot of work ahead of me with this contest, remember?"

The contest. Chris looked at her with interest. "How's that going?"

She brightened, her enthusiasm budding now that the focus was off her and on work. He wondered if all her enthusiasm was reserved for her son and her business. "The response has been great." Her gratitude was in her eyes. "I really can't thank you enough for getting me that discount. I couldn't have advertised on the air without it."

He smiled expansively, turning another part of her into Jell-O. If he remained here long enough, he would systematically reduce all of her into a quivering glob by three o'clock, she judged.

"Hey," he echoed what she had told him after letting him use her telephone, "what are neighbors for?"

*For daydreaming about.*

Her mind was wandering again, she thought. It was all Teri's fault. There was no future in thinking about Chris in any capacity except a nice neighbor. If she ever went out with him she knew it would be a disaster. Twice was enough to convince her that as far as dates went, she had two left feet. Besides, he was out of her league, anyway. What would a hunky celebrity want with her?

"So," Rosemary turned toward the dog. "Why don't you show me what this bundle of trouble can do besides chew and christen everything she comes in contact with?"

# 3

Rosemary looked at the form in front of her on the desk. She had already gone over it several times, analyzing the answers and carefully studying them.

She could generally get a feeling about people from the way they responded to the twenty-five questions on her form. She'd gotten her master's in English and had a good feel for words. In addition, she had minored in psychology. She felt that, plus her own natural intuitiveness, gave her a slight edge in discovering just what it was that made different people tick.

It worked for her as long as she wasn't personally involved. Her natural abilities had failed her when she'd made herself the subject of a match.

Maybe, she mused, her heart really hadn't been in it. Kind, considerate, handsome, and warmly funny, Patrick was a hard act to follow. Maybe her standards were too high.

Or maybe she was just a dud as a date.

But as long as she was arranging affairs for others, things went along beautifully. Her success rate was approximately seventy-three percent so far. Not everyone completed and mailed back the postcards she sent out after the initial date had taken place. But judging from the postcards that had been returned, her service and her instincts were a rousing success.

Rosemary had kept all the letters of gratitude written to her and had even been invited to three weddings. It reinforced her faith in her own shrewd abilities.

She pursed her lips, studying the form again. It had been filled out by Tommy's mother, the boy whose letter she had liked so much. If she didn't know any better, Rosemary would have sworn that *she* had been the one who had answered the questions. Tommy's mother, Mary, had tastes and preferences that were identical to her own.

If she closed her eyes, she could hear Teri asking her if there wasn't someone for her in that collection of would-be suitors she had filed away behind her. Matching Mary Smith—oh, God, was there really someone out there with such a phony-sounding name?—up with someone would almost be like matching herself up. If the match worked, it would be like living out a fantasy or having a vicarious experience.

All the gain and none of the pain, she thought, tapping short, rounded nails on her desk as she stared at the application.

Of course, the woman really wasn't her and she wouldn't be along on the date, so she'd have no way of knowing firsthand how things went. Still, it might be fun, just for the moment, to pretend that this was her own form she had in her hand.

Just who would she want to go out with?

Rosemary leaned back in her chair, rolling the idea over in her mind. If she could chose anyone, not just one of the men in the forms that were so neatly filed in the cabinet behind her, who would she really like to go out with?

Who out of the available men in her sphere...

"Atta girl, Rocky. Good girl."

Rosemary started. The deep male voice abruptly broke her concentration, taking her out of misty isles and bringing her back to her sunlit kitchen. She heard the deep rumble of male laughter. It was coming from her backyard.

Who...

The next moment she realized that the voice belonged to Chris. Tilting her chair back on its hind legs, she could just make him out. He was squatting down in her yard, patiently working with Rocky. Danny hovered in attendance, shifting from side to side, trying to help, trying to learn. Eager to join in and be useful.

Rosemary righted her chair. Danny must have coerced Chris into coming over again, sneaking out to his yard via the side gate. That made four times in as many days that Chris had been over. Rosemary felt guilty. The man had a life of his own.

Usually with some tiny-waisted, large-chested model type, she thought. Over the past few months she'd seen several different women at his side, either coming or going from the house. There were rarely repeaters.

Not that it was any of her business, Rosemary told herself.

Tired, drawn by the laughter of both her son and the man who had befriended him, she rose and drifted over toward the screened sliding back door. She needed a little break. She'd been at this all morning.

Chris was hunkered down on the lawn, trying to get Rocky to lay down flat on command. Rosemary watched, a smile forming. She bet he didn't have any trouble getting his dates to do that.

Rosemary leaned a shoulder against the inside of the doorjamb, eyeing Chris appreciatively. That man could hunker down better than anyone she'd ever seen. His jeans, well-worn and faded, were molded to a very firm posterior.

His glistening body, incredibly muscular and temptingly naked, flashed through her mind. Every fiber within her frame tightened like a clenched fist.

No, she realized, more like a spring waiting for release.

Her spring hadn't been released in a long, long time. So long, she thought, watching him lean over and straighten Rocky's paws, that it was probably completely rusted by now.

Rosemary shook her head, curtailing the thought before it could develop any further. She was fine, just fine. This wasn't the era of free love, or the "me" generation. This was the decade of restraint, of waiting until you found the right one before you warmed any sheets.

Unconsciously, she fanned herself, feeling unaccountably warm.

Rosemary sighed as she dragged her hand through her hair. Maybe she did need to get out more, to a gym or someplace like that. A little exercise would do the trick. That's what she'd do, enroll in a gym, get rid of this pent-up energy that was building within.

*After* this Mother's Day thing was resolved.

Enough procrastination, she thought, forcing herself back to her desk.

Sitting, she glanced at the form again. It was the only one she had left to deal with. She had already reviewed all the other winners' forms, matched them with suitable dates and then sent them off. After initially perusing the form, she had purposely saved this one for last, treating it the way she'd treated her meals as a child. Saving the best for last as a reward.

Out of the corner of her eye Rosemary saw Chris rise to his feet. He dusted off his hands, carelessly brushing them on the rear of his jeans.

*Him,* she thought suddenly, the idea occurring to her like a revelation. If she were in the market for a man, if she were Mary Smith, she'd choose him. Christopher Maverick. He was good-looking, patient . . . And Teri was right. His laugh did make you feel as if warm rainwater was falling on your skin.

God, she needed a cold shower.

"Okay, Mary Smith," she murmured to the form on her desk, "if that is your real name, I am about to do you a tremendous favor."

The only problem that remained now was getting Chris to agree to this. She could ask him outright to participate in the contest. After all, his radio program was already involved and he had been the one to plug the contest on the air.

Rosemary rocked in her chair, seriously toying with the approach. He might go for it. She already knew that he was easygoing and game. If he wasn't, he wouldn't be here right now, spending a Saturday afternoon with his neighbor's son.

She knew for a fact that he was unattached. The steady stream of different women he squired attested to that. What was another one more or less?

What was she thinking? Rosemary upbraided herself. This wasn't a 'more or less' situation. Though she was doing it for publicity, the end result wasn't a publicity stunt, she reminded herself. She was after genuine matches for these ten single women, just as she was for all the people who filled out applications with Soulmates, Inc.

Chris wouldn't be interested in having himself set up with someone who ultimately wanted a lasting relationship. She was sure it just wouldn't work out.

Still, she thought as she chewed thoughtfully on her pencil, Mary Smith's answers were so close to ones that she would have given, they were eerie. On top of that, they matched the few things she knew about Chris Maverick.

Maybe...

He laughed again at something Danny said to him and she felt a flutter pass over her. Warm, like the touch of a lover's hand.

Oh, what the hell? What did she have to lose by asking? She had already come to the conclusion that she wasn't satisfied matching Mary up with any of the unattached men in her existing files. The deadline was almost here. She had to set this up and get things going before she was out of time. Mother's Day was in a week.

Nothing ventured, nothing gained. Shoving her hands into the back pockets of her white cut-off denim shorts, Rosemary walked out into the backyard like Galahad set on winning the Holy Grail—if Galahad had been five-two and wearing a lime green tank top instead of a coat of heavy iron.

Chris, his arms wrapped around sheer puppy energy, glanced in her direction as he heard the screen door creak open. He almost squeezed Rocky a little too hard before setting her down again. For a short woman, Rosemary Gallagher had the longest legs he'd ever seen. The frayed shorts she wore seemed to make them look even longer. Sleeker.

He felt his appetite whetting.

Even so, he wasn't the type of man to push. Ever. He had already set out feelers around her once and she had made it clear that she wasn't interested in him that way. He supposed that there was a good side to that. It would have been awkward living next door to her after the relationship ended.

And it would end. They all did. Chris was too much of a realist to think that enduring marriages like the one his parents had actually existed in this day and age. None of the relationships he'd ever had gave any indication of lasting beyond a short stretch of time. And they never did.

Everything was disposable and transient these days. From disposable diapers to meals in a minute, everything was used and discarded. The same seemed to be true of marriages. Several of his friends had gotten married and had been divorced within a few years of the ceremony. One marriage had lasted only six months before it dissolved like a cheap paper towel trying to mop up a huge spill.

That route wasn't for him.

Still, he mused as he watched Rosemary approach him, if he ever found that one old-fashioned girl who was still out there—or old-fashioned woman, Chris amended silently—he might be tempted to give a lasting relationship one hell of a shot.

"I didn't realize that you were here," Rosemary began, testing the waters slowly. He lifted a shoulder and let it drop. She'd never realized what a sexy gesture that was.

"I'm sorry, I didn't mean to just barge in, but Danny—"

She shook her head, cutting his apology short. "I was just about to apologize to you for Danny roping you into this." Rosemary nodded at Rocky.

"Mom," Danny protested. "I didn't rope him. He wanted to help."

"That's right," Chris agreed. "There was no roping involved." His smile was engaging and so sensual Rosemary dug her fingernails into her palms. "I told you before, I like this."

He grinned at Danny. Rocky was nipping at his boots but he seemed oblivious to it. "It reminds me of when I was a kid." He looked around the postage-stamp-size enclosed lot, remembering the one without boundaries where he had run free. "There were always dogs all over the place." His eyes shifted to Rosemary. "I'm too busy these days to keep a dog of my own, so I thought I might just adopt Rocky part-time. If you didn't mind?"

Rocky was still busy licking Chris's boots, turning them a darker brown, and wiggling her bottom.

Rosemary laughed. "I don't mind, and it's easy to see that Rocky doesn't." She watched as Rocky's tail waved eagerly. "You always have this effect on females?"

He liked the way she laughed. Her eyes crinkled and the sound was soft and sultry. "They don't generally piddle at my feet," he remarked, discreetly leaving the question unanswered.

Chris covertly transferred the dog treats he had in his back pocket to Danny. The boy took them eagerly, waiting for instruction. "Show your mother what Rocky's learned."

Danny's head bobbed up and down. "Hey, yeah, watch this, Mom."

"Why don't you stand over here?" Chris suggested. Placing his hands on her hips, he physically moved her next to him. The feel of his hands didn't exactly help her maintain a tight grip on that rusted spring of hers, she thought ruefully.

Trying to focus on what Danny was doing, Rosemary watched the unruly puppy actually come when she was called, sit up and then lie down. Danny insisted on performing each trick twice. It was hard to tell who was more eager, Danny or the puppy.

Rosemary applauded dutifully at the end of the miniperformance.

"Very impressive." She turned toward Chris. "Now if you could just get her to stop using the house as one big bathroom—"

She saw that her words sparked something within his memory. He took her hand. "That reminds me, I brought you something."

If anything, she would have expected him to bring something for Danny. "Me?"

He laughed, clearing his throat. "Well, it's for Rocky, really. But in a roundabout way, it is actually for you."

He had her intrigued. "Okay, I'll bite. No pun intended, Rocky," she said, glancing at the dog. "What did you bring for Rocky that I can use, too?"

"It's more for your peace of mind." Chris laughed as confusion deepened on her face. "C'mon, I'll show you."

Still holding her hand, he led her through the open side gate into his own backyard. The screen door was still standing open and he walked into the house. Danny brought up the rear with Rocky trotting adoringly behind all of them.

Rosemary had just managed to curve her hand in his when he dropped it and gestured toward the large, flat box leaning against the black-and-gray sofa in his family room. "I picked this up on my way home this afternoon. I was doing a benefit show in the mall."

She looked from the box to Chris. "You brought her a box?" Rocky had already made confetti out of two oatmeal boxes, an empty doggie treat box and one shoe box—with shoes. "It's big, but it's not entirely unique."

"No." Taking her hand again, he led her to the front of the box. There was a drawing of a puppy sitting within a large wire cage. The puppy was smiling. "I brought her a puppy cage." He tapped the drawing. "This way, she's not all over the house while Danny's in school."

It was as if the sun had suddenly come out. Rosemary looked at the drawing in fascination. In the past week she'd spent most of her time following a dog around that seemed to be all teeth, intent on sampling everything within the house at least twice.

She looked at Chris. "Are you applying for sainthood?"

"The form's already signed and in the mail." The grin on his lips didn't belong to any saint, living or dead. It was guaranteed to raise temperatures ten to fifteen degrees if she was any judge.

Rosemary tried not to notice how much his smile melted every solid thing in her. It was a fruitless attempt. She wondered if Mary Smith would name her first child after her.

"Speaking of forms..." Rosemary began tentatively. "I was wondering—"

"Hey, Chris," Danny broke in. "I got her to jump up." He held up his hand, freshly denuded of the treat he had been holding to tempt Rocky to follow through. Rocky jumped a second time on command, hoping for another reward. A whimper followed when there was none.

Chris nodded his approval. "Very good."

He sounded as if he meant it. The man was a find, she thought, pleased. Now, if she could only get him to agree to go out with Tommy's mother, everything would be wonderful. She opened her mouth to continue with her pitch when Danny interrupted again.

Danny pointed to the long, flat carton, his brows drawn together in one blond, wiggly line as he studied it. "What's that?"

Christ bent down to let Rocky lick his fingers, then scratched the dog behind the ears. "Rocky's new home. So that your mother can get some work done in peace while you're in school."

Danny cocked his head, studying the drawing. "How does it work?"

"C'mon." Chris picked the box up. "Let's take it over to your house and I'll set it up for you." He raised the box and balanced it partially against his shoulder as he nodded toward the doorway. Danny scurried in front of him, opening the front door and holding it. He managed to grab Rocky just before she darted out.

Rosemary was careful to remain behind Chris and out of range. She closed his door, then caught up to him on her front step. Danny was ahead of them. He threw the door open for Chris a moment before he reached it. She winced as she heard the doorknob make contact with the wall. Plaster. She had to remember to pick up plaster.

"How much do I owe you for the cage?" She glanced at the wall as she closed the door. There was a faint halo of white forming where the doorknob had hit. Always something, she thought.

"Nothing." He set the box down in the living room. "Consider it payment for the pleasure of playing with your dog."

He certainly knew how to be charming, she thought. "You're training my dog," Rosemary corrected. "I should be paying you for that, too."

"Okay." He turned abruptly. When he looked at her, Rosemary suddenly felt her mouth grow dry. "How about dinner?"

"'Dinner'?" she echoed as if the word was completely foreign to her.

There were those signals again, he thought. She looked as if he had just proposed that she go bareback riding on a shark. For a second, when she had been in his yard, he had thought that they were finally on a different footing. But it looked as if he had misread her. Again.

Chris shrugged carelessly as he pulled the tabs apart on one side of the carton. "Just a thought—"

Dinner. He was talking about food, not a date. What was she thinking? He had those gorgeous women flitting in and out of his house. He certainly didn't need to make a date with her if he wanted companionship.

"Sure, why not?"

He looked at her in surprise. She'd certainly changed her mind in a hurry.

"Tonight." She stopped, trying to remember what was in her refrigerator. "I was planning on making pot roast—" It was Danny's favorite and he had been begging her for it all week.

Chris leaned the box against the sofa and slowly pulled out four long pieces of metal and two shorter ones. They clanked as they settled on her light green carpet. "With small potatoes?"

For a second he looked just like a hungry little boy. Rosemary laughed, feeling infinitely more relaxed. "As small as you like."

Carefully, he laid out the bottom piece and hooked first one side, then the other onto it. "You're on." Satisfied that the wire walls were secure, he reached for the top section. Danny scurried around him and got to it first. With a smile worthy of a toothpaste commercial, he handed the piece to Chris. "What time do you want me over?"

She did a quick calculation. If she put the roast into the oven within the next hour, that would give her enough time to clean the place up a little. "Six?"

He nodded. "Six it is." Chris glanced over his shoulder at the instruction sheet. He didn't like to read step-by-step directions, but studying a picture always seemed to do the trick for him. "All right, everything seems to be in order. Let's slide in the bottom tray and have Rocky try out her new home."

With the dog running circles around them, Chris and Danny secured the tray. It ran along the length and breadth of the bottom of the cage. At least the rug under it would stay clean, she thought.

Rosemary studied what Chris had just constructed. It looked like a cage, all right. Just like the ones in the pet shops where sad-eyed puppies laid around listlessly all day. Only much larger. She glanced at him uncertainly. This was her first dog and he had had many, so she guessed he knew what he was doing. Still, she had to ask, just for her own peace of mind.

"Um, isn't that kind of cruel, keeping her in a cage like that?"

She was softhearted. He liked that. A lot of women he'd come across didn't care about animals.

"No, they tend to treat it like a den." He swung open the cage door. "All dogs are basically wild animals—"

The shiver came involuntarily as she crossed her arms across her chest. "Thanks, I needed to hear that. I'm already envisioning bared teeth sinking into my neck."

"Mom—"

Chris tried not to notice how her cleavage deepened when she crossed her arms like that. With effort, he concentrated on what she was saying. "You're afraid of dogs?"

She nodded.

He didn't understand. What was she doing with a dog, especially one that appeared to be a German shepherd mix, if she was afraid of them.

"Then why—"

The answer was so simple, she didn't understand what the confusion was.

"Because Danny wants one so much and right now she's a puppy." Rosemary glanced at the dog. Rocky seemed to be growing right before her eyes. "I was hoping to get used to her slowly so that by the time she's a large dog, I won't feel threatened."

Somehow she had her doubts about that, but she could hope for the best.

"Interesting," he murmured, rolling her theory over in his head. He could attach several applications to it, and one very pertinent one. "Very in-ter-esting."

She laughed at the way he drew out the word. "There was a comedian who used to say that on an old TV show—"

"Yes, I know. 'Laugh-In.'"

She stared at him, stunned. "You watched 'Laugh-In'?"

He nodded. "My parents used to watch it. I've got an old video I found in this store that deals in hard-to-find tapes. It's great stuff."

Something else in common. With both her and Mary Smith. "Yeah, it was." She watched as Rocky slowly investigated this newest addition to the living room. Several sniffs later, she wandered into the cage.

"Leave the door open for a while," he told Danny, "until she gets used to it. You don't want her to think she's being punished. After a while, you can just close it. She'll think of it as her home within a home."

Rosemary didn't know what to say. He seemed to be the answer to a prayer. "Chris, you've been really terrific about everything."

He winked at her. "Terrific's my middle name."

No argument there, she thought. Well, now or never. "I was wondering if maybe you'd be up to doing me another favor."

He sat cross-legged on the floor. Danny settled in beside him, attempting to mimic him.

"Oh, such as what?" He scratched Rocky on her belly. The dog raised both front paws in the air and looked as if she were in ecstasy.

"Well, I have this application form from that Mother's Day contest." She hesitated.

Chris stopped scratching Rocky and looked up, waiting. "Yes?"

Rosemary plunged ahead. "She sounds as if you and she like the same things."

Chris studied her. What was she driving at? "I didn't fill out an application," he reminded her.

She wet her lips. "Yes, I know, but from what you've told me, it sounds as if the two of you have a lot in common." He was looking at her so intently with those green eyes of his that she was losing her train of thought. "And I thought that perhaps you might consider..." Her voice trailed off, evaporating in a dry mouth.

"Going out with her?" he completed.

She nodded. Maybe if she made him think it was simply part of the publicity stunt, he might agree to it. Once they were on the date, things could work themselves out.

She tried again, summoning all her persuasive powers. "You know, you could perhaps even research the matter, dating in the nineties while playing music from the sixties, something like that."

"You mean, date her for the show?"

He was going to say no, she thought. "Never mind, bad idea." She turned to move away, sorry that she had even suggested it.

He caught her wrist. "No." He'd said the word slowly, as if he were digesting it. Damn, but his eyes were mesmerizing. "It's not really a bad idea at all." He grinned. "Sure, why not. Match me up to your single mom. It might be fun at that."

He totally disarmed her. "You really are a very good sport, Chris."

He rose to his feet. Danny and Rocky immediately jumped to theirs. "Hey, that's my other middle name."

Danny looked at him, puzzled. "How many middle names do you have?"

Chris ruffled his hair, then slid his hands into his front pockets. "We'll go over them later." He frowned slightly. Danny was trying to push Rocky into the cage. "No, not like that, Danny. You can't make her stay. That'll only frighten her. We don't want to do that. Sometimes you'll find that things have to be gently coaxed along."

Chris glanced at Rosemary over his shoulder and then smiled.

# 4

**"H**appy Mother's Day!"

The shouted greeting echoed in Rosemary's head as she pried her eyes open. She managed to jerk her head off the pillow just as Rocky bounded on top of her bed. The puppy was immediately followed by Danny. She was bracketed between the two of them.

Blinking as her heart stopped pounding and slowly slid back down her throat, Rosemary focused on the digital clock next to her bed.

Seven a.m. So much for wild, frivolous thoughts of sleeping in.

But there were better things than sleep, she thought, like the warm, enthusiastic hug of a child. Rosemary sighed blissfully as Danny wrapped his arms around her and squeezed tight.

"Thank you, sweetheart." Rocky, her tail thumping madly against the goose down comforter, was busy licking her arm. Rosemary looked over Danny's head at the dog. "You too, Rocky."

The dog barked several times in response to the sound of her name.

Rosemary laughed, gingerly wiping her arm. "Well, at least she knows who she is, which is more than I do at this hour on a Sunday."

Danny looked puzzled, not knowing why the day of the week would have anything to do with knowing who you were. He slid off the bed, dragging a little of the comforter after him. Rosemary discreetly tugged it back up.

"I wanted to wake you up early so that you could get ready."

Rosemary cast one last, longing glance at her pillow. The next moment Rocky plopped her muzzle down on it. Time for laundry, she thought.

Mustering an interested smile, Rosemary dragged her hand through her hair and looked at Danny. "Ready for what?"

He was so excited, he looked as if he was positively going to burst. "I'm going to take you out."

Her little man. Did it get any better than this? *We've got a great kid, Patrick.*

She reached over and touched his cheek affectionately. Rocky yipped and jumped from the bed, hovering protectively around Danny. Rosemary gave the dog a stern look, the way Chris had instructed her to do when Rocky attempted to assert herself. He'd warned her that the puppy would try to up her position in the food chain by challenging her as well as Danny.

*Tough, dog. He was mine first.*

"Oh, honey, I don't want you spending your allowance on me."

Danny's grin grew wider. "It's okay, Mom. If I run out of money, you have some, right?"

These were the nineties, all right. It was a toss-up these days who paid for the "date." Danny was going to have an easy time of it when it was his turn to date.

"Right." She laughed and rested her chin on her raised knees. "So, where are you taking me, or is it a surprise?"

Danny's face seemed to brighten even more, if that were possible. It was as if she had just solved a problem for him, she mused.

"It's a surprise."

She pretended to go along and look perplexed. "Then how will we get there? Can we walk?"

He shook his head. "No, but I'll give you directions when we're in the car."

This should be very interesting, Rosemary thought. As a pathfinder, Danny was a great baseball player. His sense of direction was rivaled only by hers. She'd long since ceased being embarrassed by the fact that she always seemed to get lost whenever she ventured someplace new. At this point in her life, it was a given, and she simply allotted more time when she had to travel to a new destination.

He was taking this so seriously, it was all she could do to keep from hugging him again. "Is there any special time that we have to leave?"

"Eleven." The puppy jumped at him and he gave her a sign that meant she should sit. He repeated it three times before she obeyed. "No, maybe we'd better go at ten-thirty so we can get there in time."

The time struck a chord. Eleven o'clock was when Chris was supposed to meet Tommy Smith's mother. Teri had handled the arrangements. Rosemary wasn't aware that she was smiling as she thought of the dinner she'd shared with Chris last week. Danny had been there with them, so it couldn't be construed as a date, but it had been nice, very nice...

No, there was no point in thinking about that now. She'd done her part. She had set the date up and now she would just have to forget about it, unless there were disastrous consequences to deal with.

Still, if she were being completely honest with herself, there was a tiny part of her that felt just the teensiest bit... jealous, she supposed.

*About what, Rosemary? If he actually asked you out, you'd be the first one running for the hills.*

She pushed all thoughts of Chris and his date out of her mind and concentrated on her own "date." "This is all very mysterious, Danny."

He grinned from ear to ear, pleased at her comment. "Yeah."

Well, he was obviously enjoying all this, and that was her real gift, she thought. Seeing Danny happy. Even if it meant driving to some unknown destination or spending her days putting up with an overly

energetic dog that thought of her house as one great
big chew toy.

Rosemary looked at Rocky as she scooted her off
the bed, where she had managed to scramble up again.
Basically, she had to admit that Chris had done a
wonderful job with the animal so far. Rocky responded to her name, did a handful of amusing tricks
and had actually hit upon the fact that the house was
not just one great big bathroom waiting for her deposit.

And the cage he'd brought them was nothing short
of a godsend. She could actually leave the dog in the
house and know that she wouldn't find shredded
drapes when she returned.

Rosemary swung her legs out of the bed and nar-
rowly avoided having her toes nipped. Danny pulled
back his pet. Nipping was something Chris had yet to
work out for her.

This wasn't right, she upbraided herself. She had to
handle this by herself. She wasn't supposed to be de-
pending on Chris for help. But she had to admit that
it did make matters a lot easier for her . . .

Rosemary crossed to her closet and slid the mir-
rored door back. "Anything special that you'd like me
to wear to this mysterious place you're taking me to,
oh, young sir?"

Danny pursed his lips together in a manner that said
"Oh, Mom," but he refrained from saying it out loud.
He actually appeared to be giving her question seri-
ous thought.

Rosemary suppressed a smile. She didn't want him to think she was laughing at him. But he did look adorable. He was getting to be so grown up, she mused, feeling the bittersweet sting that seemed to naturally accompany that sort of realization.

She bit her tongue to keep from saying something to that effect. He hated it when she did that. Just as she had hated it when her own parents had done it to her, she remembered. The picture was very different from the other side of the frame.

*Sorry, Mom and Dad. I never knew that you felt this way.*

Danny came to stand next to her and peered into her closet. "How about your blue one?"

She looked at him, stunned. "My blue one?"

She had only one blue dress and it was hardly what she would have picked to wear when going out with her son. It was a cocktail dress, cut rather low in the front and scooped out down to her waist in the back. She'd worn it exactly once, a year ago, to a friend's wedding, and then had retired it to the side of her closet. The dress was far too form-fitting and revealing for an afternoon outing with her son.

"Yeah." Danny looked at the dress, pushing the other dresses away from it. "You look sexy in it." Danny gave the impression that he was forcing the word out of his mouth.

And just who had taught him about that? Hiding her surprise, she looked at him suspiciously. "What do you know about sexy?"

He drew himself up, squaring his shoulders. "Guys think it's a good thing on a girl."

She knew Danny was growing up, but not this fast. Rosemary took his chin in her hand and looked him in the eye, hiding her amusement.

"Well, this guy is going to have to *not* think about that for a few more years, okay?"

"Okay," he sighed.

She felt a smidgen better. She'd had the necessary talk with him about sex over a year ago. He had looked a little repulsed and hadn't asked too many questions thereafter. Danny needed a man to fill in the gaps, she realized now. Maybe Teri's husband could—

No, Jim was heavy-handed about almost everything. He'd probably either find a way to scare Danny to death, or take him for a visit with a strolling lady of the evening. She was going to have to think of someone else . . .

Chris.

Funny how he had a way of popping into her head lately. But Danny got along very well with Chris. Maybe Chris could answer any lingering questions he might have and fill him in on—

Rosemary stopped herself abruptly. Maybe she'd better leave well enough alone. He was training her puppy. If she asked him to have a heart-to-heart with her son about sex, he might get the wrong idea. For the life of her, she didn't know what the right idea was anymore. The man had her engine running even if she had taken the tires off nine years ago.

Sex was a subject that she was just going to have to handle on her own. "Anything you want to talk to me about, Danny?" she asked gently.

Turning, she saw that Danny was on the floor, trying to make Rocky sit instead of nibble on the side of the bureau. The conversation about sex was tabled.

"No!" She rushed over and pulled the dog away in dismay.

"Chris hasn't finished training her." It was half an apology, half an explanation.

"So I noticed."

Rosemary returned to her closet, one eye on the dog. But Rocky had rediscovered her tail and was giving it a cursory lick. Satisfied that her bureau was temporarily out of danger, Rosemary moved a few hangers around and then took out a flowered sundress.

She held it up for Danny's approval. "How about this one?"

He studied it thoughtfully, then nodded. "Okay. And could you wear your hair up? The way you did yesterday? So your neck shows?"

Now *that* was an odd request. He'd never commented on her hair before. She slid her hand along her neck. "My neck? Why do you want to see my neck?"

Danny shrugged carelessly, tickling the dog's stomach. "Chris said it was pretty."

"He did?" Rosemary's pulse quickened just a tad. *A little late for that, isn't it? You matched him up with another woman, remember?* "All right, if that's what you want." She pointed toward the door. "Now take Rocky out and scoot. I want to take a shower."

Danny rose to his feet, holding Rocky. The dog was dangling over his arms like a boneless cat. He stopped in the doorway and looked over his shoulder at her bureau. "Can you wear that smelly stuff, too?"

Rosemary drew her brows together. "'Smelly stuff'?" she echoed.

Danny backtracked to her bureau. Moving a couple of jars around, he picked up a small bottle of perfume, then thrust it into her hand. "This."

Was this her Danny? He was certainly giving her an awful lot of prerequisites for this "date" of theirs. She could just envision him when he really started dating girls.

Just what was it that he and Chris talked about so intently while they trained Rocky? She certainly didn't want Danny growing up any faster than he already was.

Her hand curved around the bottle. "Okay, pretty dress, hair up, smelly stuff. Anything else?"

"I'll let you know," he said importantly as he walked out.

Definitely growing up too fast, she thought as she closed the door.

At exactly ten-thirty on the nose, Danny had a death grip on her hand and was dragging her out to the driveway and their car.

"What's the rush, honey? Do we have reservations?" He looked at her blankly as she unlocked her car. "Apparently not." Rosemary got in and waited until he was buckled in. "All right, I'm ready." She placed her key into the ignition and turned it, then looked at him expectantly. "So, where to?"

Danny debated on how much to tell her. "Down the block."

That would take them several hundred feet. "And then?"

He opened his mouth, then shut it, taking a deep breath. "I'll tell you when we get there."

She'd be driving in fits and starts. And wouldn't the Bedford police love that one? She could celebrate Mother's Day by getting a ticket for going too slow.

"Danny, I'd really feel a lot better if you told me where we were going." She saw the stubborn look that entered his eyes. That he had gotten from his father, she thought. "I'm going to find out where it is when we get there. A few minutes earlier won't really matter, will it?"

"No, I guess not." He sighed, then relented. "The Big Soda Shoppe."

Rosemary stared at him. That was where Chris was supposed to meet Tommy Smith's mother. He knew that. She'd told him because it was his favorite place to go and she'd thought it was an incredible coincidence.

"Danny, we can't go there. Chris is meeting Mary there. You know, Tommy's mother? If we show up, it'll look like we're spying."

Danny gave her a soulful look that he knew always got to his mother. He saved it for special pleas. "But it's my favorite place, and yours, too. You said so. They play all those old songs you like and it looks just like that place on 'Happy Days.'"

Everything he said was true, but she still didn't want to go. She had no desire to see Chris out with someone else, even if she had arranged it. She glanced at Danny and his pout deepened, weakening her resolve.

She supposed that it wasn't that small a place. They could get a table somewhere in the corner, away from Chris and his date. He didn't even have to see her if she was careful—

Great, now she was turning into a Peeping Thomasina. "Honey, I really don't think that we should—" Danny's eyes grew sadder as his lower lip protruded even further. Any more and he could use it as a rain catcher. Teri was right. She was a pushover. "Oh, all right, I suppose he probably won't even see us."

Danny beamed. "Great!"

*Yeah, great.*

"We'll see just how great," she murmured. With an inward sigh, she turned the car onto the main drag and drove South.

* * *

When they walked into The Big Soda Shoppe twenty minutes later, Rosemary spotted Chris immediately. He was seated, very much alone, at a booth near the front door. There were more than a few booths empty at this hour. With any luck, they could slide into one before Chris looked their way.

Rosemary glanced at her watch. It was five to eleven. The woman was obviously one of those people who arrived on the dot.

"Hey, there's Chris," Danny announced loudly, pointing him out.

"Yes," she hissed softly, hoping that Danny would take her lead and lower his voice. "I know."

His fingers wound in hers—an oddity that she hadn't explored yet since Danny hated to hold hands—he began to drag her toward Chris's booth. "Let's say hello."

But she refused to budge. "Danny, we can't just walk up to him. He's on a date."

Danny shook his head adamantly, gesturing with his free hand toward the booth. "But she's not here yet. We can say hi, can't we? Look, he's seen us."

Small wonder, she thought. Danny was practically shouting above the music.

"Didn't you say it was rude to ignore people?" Danny persisted.

Served her right for enforcing etiquette to such a degree.

"Yes, I did." There was nothing left to do but walk over to Chris's booth. She pasted on a smile as she approached.

Chris rose slightly in his seat, his gaze fixed on Rosemary. Though he had a sweet tooth, Rosemary looked far more tempting than anything he was going to find on the menu. He'd never seen her wearing anything other than shorts and skimpy tops before. The dress she had on swirled around her legs as she walked and seemed to float along her hips like a multicolored cloud. She was wearing her hair piled up on her head, exposing a soft, ivory column that left his mouth dry.

She looked nervous, he thought, and wondered why.

"We're not here to spy, honest," Rosemary blurted before she could phrase her apology more gracefully. "Danny insisted on bringing me here for Mother's Day. It's his favorite place."

"Excellent choice," he told Danny. "I'm very partial to ice cream myself, and they've got a great selection of music available." He nodded at the tiny jukeboxes that were the hallmark of each booth. "Would you like to sit down?" He gestured to the empty seats across from him.

Rosemary was very tempted, but she shook her head. It wouldn't be right. "I don't think I should be sitting with you. I mean, when your date arrives, I don't think she's banking on a foursome."

Danny was already way ahead of her and blocked her argument. He pointed to the adjacent booth. "But we can sit down in the next booth, can't we, Mom? Then we can talk to Chris until she gets here."

Without waiting for her reply, he planted his bottom on the seat and twisted around so that he could look at Chris while he talked.

Rosemary bit her lip. She could just guess what was going through Chris's head. "This is really very awkward."

But he smiled and seemed to take it all in stride. "Why don't you sit down with Danny? I could use the company."

She sincerely doubted that, but he was being so nice about it that she couldn't very well say no. Rosemary slid in opposite her son. Chris sat down in his booth, draping one arm over the side and turning his body so that he could face them.

"Well, I set this up and she is late. I guess I owe you a little company until she arrives." Rosemary looked sternly at her son. "But once she gets here, we're moving to another table, got that?"

Danny nodded solemnly, his baby fine hair bobbing up and down around his head.

Chris toyed with the straw in his ice-cream soda. Rosemary noted that the whipped cream had faded into the drink. He'd been here awhile.

"So, how's your Mother's Day going so far?" he asked her.

"Rocky sat up and rolled over three times for her," Danny announced before she could answer.

Rosemary spread her hands out, as if to indicate that her plate was full. "What more could any mother ask for?" She laughed easily.

Her eyes crinkled a little when she laughed. He thought it was cute. And she was delicious. "I could think of a few things."

The implication in his voice had Rosemary's imagination taking wing. She curbed it, but not quickly enough. She felt her cheeks growing pink again and damned herself for her fair complexion.

"I really can't," she lied, looking down at the printed menu tucked against the jukebox.

*Yes, she could,* he thought, smiling to himself. "Wasn't this scene in *Separate Tables,* or something?"

Rosemary raised her eyes from the menu. "You watch old movies?"

He nodded as if that was a given. "Only kind worth watching." Chris could tell by her expression that she agreed with him. Warming to his subject, he leaned closer. "You know, the university shows some terrific old classics every Friday at their theater. Would you be interested in going with me this Friday?"

The easy atmosphere burst apart like a soap bubble drifting in the wind. She shook her head. "Sorry, I'm busy."

There was that signal again. But this time he pushed just a little. "Next Friday?"

She shook her head. "No, I promised Teri I'd baby-sit her twins."

Danny looked at his mother, surprised. This was news to him.

Chris picked up the quizzical look on the boy's face. He lifted a shoulder and then let it drop. "Maybe some other time."

"Maybe." Her smile felt a little too tight. The waitress approached her table. She was never so relieved to see a stranger in her life.

Danny hadn't even bothered looking at the menu. He had been planning this all week. "Two Kitchen Sinks with the works."

So saying, he looked hopefully at his mother.

If he had one of his own, he would be sick all night. Still, she couldn't turn him down completely. She tried not to think about her arteries screaming in self-defense. "How about one Kitchen Sink with two spoons?"

Danny glanced at Chris. "Maybe three?"

She was beginning to wonder who was the match-maker in the family, her or Danny. "Mr. Maverick is waiting for someone, remember?" Rosemary glanced at her watch. "Someone who's late."

Rosemary hated that more than anything. She had always thought it was the height of rudeness to keep anybody else waiting.

Danny looked at Chris, hoping for corroboration. "Just until she shows up," he agreed. "They're really something else," he told Chris.

"I'm sure they are." Chris looked at Rosemary, his eyes meeting hers. "Maybe I'll just have a taste when it arrives."

"Provided your date hasn't," Rosemary felt honor bound to interject.

"Provided my date hasn't," he echoed, his smile reaching up to his eyes and then flowing to hers.

His eyes were the most beautiful shade of green, Rosemary thought a second before she roused herself. She wasn't supposed to be having thoughts about him now, while he was waiting for another woman. A woman she had set him up with.

She could just hear Teri berating her. "God, Rosemary, what are you giving away?"

But he wasn't hers to give away. She was just doing what she always did, trying to bring a little joy into other people's lives. Arranging other people's happiness. Other people who didn't seize up and then get a deep, burning, sinking sensation in the pit of their stomach at the very mention of the word "date."

"Three spoons it is," she said as cheerfully as she could manage. She looked up at the waitress, who wasn't looking at her at all. Her eyes and a very inviting smile were fixed on Chris. "We'll have a Kitchen Sink," Rosemary told the woman, "any time you're ready."

"I'm ready now," the waitress purred, still looking at Chris. "Say," she asked suddenly, "aren't you the guy on the bus?"

He shook his head. "I never take the bus."

"No, I meant—oh, never mind," she mumbled. "That was a Kitchen Sink?" she asked Rosemary.

"With three spoons," Danny piped up.

"With three spoons," the woman muttered, walking away. She looked over her shoulder at Chris again and then shook her head, as if trying to summon a memory.

# 5

—→ ←—

"Here you go, one Soda Shoppe Kitchen Sink with three spoons."

Balancing the huge concoction of pinks, greens, whites and assorted colors in between, the waitress carefully slid the teeming dish of ice cream from the tray onto the table. She moved it to the center of the table, then deposited the silverware beside it. Sparing Chris one long, wistful look, she retreated to take other orders.

Danny leaned over and picked up a spoon. But instead of digging into the mountain of ice cream the way Rosemary expected him to, he scrambled off his seat, all legs and wiggly parts. He looked not unlike Rocky, Rosemary thought.

He waved the utensil in front of an amused Chris. "Here's your spoon, Chris. You can have that taste now."

That had to be the biggest plate of ice cream he had ever seen, Chris decided. He gave a cursory glance toward the door. A man and a woman entered, preceded by four children. Satisfied, Chris rose.

"Scoot over," he told Danny.

But Danny sank down in his seat, firmly replanting his bottom.

"Um, it's a little sticky over here." He nodded toward his side of the bench. "Maybe you'd better sit down next to Mom." The suggestion was tendered a little too brightly. "I don't want to get my good pants dirty."

Rosemary raised a brow. Now *this* was something new. Since when had Danny begun to notice that he was a dirt magnet? Or care?

Chris was standing at her elbow, waiting. "Do you mind?"

From this angle, he looked so tall, so sexy. So overwhelming. For a split second she froze before coming to life.

"No, of course not." Rosemary shifted over, giving him room. His leg brushed against hers as he seated himself. He left it there, as if he wasn't aware that their limbs were touching. Rosemary's heart skipped a beat.

This was all so crazy. One minute he was a friend, a neighbor she'd fixed up with someone she thought was his match. The next minute he was something else entirely. Someone who had her warming up and freezing up at the same time.

She had to make up her mind.

She had, she insisted silently. Chris was someone else's date and that was that. She wasn't in the dating market. She just had to keep reminding herself of that.

Completely oblivious to the internal skirmish being waged a heartbeat away from him, Chris skimmed his spoon along a mound of strawberry ice cream. It mingled with a little of the pistachio and some of the hot fudge topping. He slid the spoon into his mouth and closed his eyes, savoring the taste.

Watching, Rosemary felt herself drifting again.

Why didn't they turn up the air-conditioning in this place? The room was getting incredibly warm. She reached for her glass of water and took a long sip.

Chris looked at Danny. "Hmm, you're right. This is good."

Danny crowed in triumph. "See, I knew it. Mom likes it, too, don't you, Mom?"

Things would go a whole lot smoother if she got her mind back on the ice cream and not on the consumer. With determination, Rosemary dipped her spoon into the towering, colorful mountain, then let it melt on her tongue.

"I love it," she corrected. "If I gave in to my inclinations, I'd look like a Kitchen Sink pretty soon myself."

Purposely avoiding looking at him, Rosemary took another spoonful of dessert and let it slide down her throat.

"I don't see something like that happening for a long while."

Despite her best intentions, she raised her eyes to Chris's. They were skimming over her as lightly as his spoon had skimmed along the serving of ice cream.

And she was melting just as fast.

He was good, she thought. Very good. He could raise goose flesh on her without so much as touching her. He didn't have to.

His eyes were doing it for him.

Somehow, though it was almost paralyzed, she found her tongue. "Thanks, but you had to say that." Sinking quickly, Rosemary looked toward the front door as it opened. But it was only a little girl followed closely by her parents. No thirty-year-old woman, looking around, holding a white flower. No Mary Smith in sight.

"No, I didn't," Chris contradicted. "I don't have to say anything. I can just put some ice cream in my mouth and keep it shut."

To illustrate his point, he slid another spoonful into his mouth and then winked at her.

A flutter in her stomach responded. Damn, how could anyone look so sexy eating ice cream?

"Well, I'd better let you have a go at this before I manage to eat it all." Chris began to put down his spoon on the paper napkin and began to rise.

"You know," Danny piped up suddenly, "maybe my eyes are bigger than my stomach, just like my mom is always saying. It'd be awful to waste this." He gestured toward the plate. "Mom thinks it's a sin to waste food," he confided. "Can you stay and help us eat this? Just until your date gets here," he added quickly.

Chris looked at Rosemary warmly. "Your mom's right. It is a sin to waste food. And I never turn down a plea for help." He sat down again.

This time he looked as if he had settled in for good, Rosemary thought. But what if Mary Smith turned up? What would she think?

Rosemary looked down at her watch again. The woman was now almost half an hour late. She supposed it might serve Mary right for keeping her date waiting like this if she arrived and found him otherwise occupied.

Still, having Chris sitting here with them, waiting, wasn't exactly orthodox . . .

This, she thought, was what was known as a dilemma. A big one.

He wondered what she was thinking. And if her vocal cords had frozen yet. She was putting the ice cream away as if she was afraid that it might overflow at any moment.

As if she might say something she didn't want to if her mouth wasn't full.

Rosemary Gallagher certainly was an unusual woman. But then, he had never been really interested in the mundane and the common.

He could sense her tension. "So, how did you get into this business in the first place?"

She raised her eyes to his. "Matchmaking? It sort of found me one bleak Friday morning." She saw him raise a curious brow, but he continued eating. Continued slowly licking his spoon with a rhythm that was hopelessly sensual. Rosemary had to struggle to concentrate on her answer.

"I was going over the want ads," she explained. "I'd just lost my job at the university and I couldn't find anything suitable. It seemed that there was nothing out there for a woman with a degree in English. Anyway, the personals were located right before the employment section."

She warmed to her subject, remembering how she had felt, reading ad after ad. "It struck me that it was all so sad."

"What was?" he prodded, intrigued. For the moment that nervous, cat-on-a-hot-tin-roof look had left her. Rosemary was relaxed, softer, and devastatingly attractive this way.

"That there were so many people out there looking for each other, missing each other because they didn't really know how to go about finding that good man or good woman they felt would make their life complete." She shrugged, licking her spoon. "Personals are okay, but there's a bit of risk involved, and even computer dating misses the heart of things." She smiled to herself as she remembered. "Patrick always told me I was good at looking into people's hearts."

Chris drew his brows together. "Patrick?" Was she involved with someone after all? Was that why she had given off those no-trespassing signals when he had subtly felt her out?

"My late husband."

Her eyes had grown sad. Rosemary still loved him, he thought. Chris toyed with the few sprinkles that had drizzled down onto the side of the plate. He and Danny had systematically gotten rid of all the ones on top. "How long were you married?"

She glanced down at the ring she still wore, caressing it with her thumb. "Five years. But we were together forever."

She said it as if there was more involved than a couple just living together. "In the mystical sense?"

She laughed. Patrick would have gotten a kick out of that. He had been grounded in common sense. There hadn't been anyone more down to earth than he had been.

"In the physical sense. I grew up with Patrick. We were neighbors." *Just like we are.* Now where had that come from? She pushed the thought away. "He was always there, for as long as I could remember. We went to the same schools, had the same friends..."

She shrugged, her voice trailing off. Ice cream was a much safer subject, she thought, looking at the platter. They had certainly made a considerable dent in it. As a matter of fact, it was two-thirds gone.

"Hey, there's Jeff with his mom," Danny announced. As if his dress pants had suddenly been wired with electricity, he squirmed in his seat. "Can I go and say hi to him? I'll only be a minute," he promised.

She'd never known Danny to be that enthusiastic about Jeff before. Jeff was one of the boys in his class and on his Little League team, but they had never been what she had thought close or really good friends.

"Sure, go ahead."

Danny was off like a shot, leaving the two of them alone, chaperoned only by the dwindling mountain of ice cream, she thought.

Chris grinned as he took another spoonful. The ice cream was swiftly losing its shape. "Danny's a really neat kid."

Nothing he could have said could have warmed her heart more.

"Yes, I know." She watched as Danny headed toward Jeff's table. "He's what I'm proudest of." She didn't realize that she was sighing until it escaped her lips. "It hasn't been easy."

No, he didn't imagine that it would be. But she had done a great job. He'd been a handful and a half for his own mother and there had been times that she had exclaimed she would have lost her mind if his father had not intervened.

"How long have you been alone?"

"Too long." She looked up ruefully, aware of how that must have sounded. "Oh, don't get me wrong. I'm not lonely—I've got Danny, and now that four-footed creature following me around." She paused, trying to find the right words. "It's just that at times it would be nice to have a man for Danny to talk to."

Was that the only reason she wanted someone around? To talk to her son? "How about you, Rosemary? Do you need a man to talk to?"

He'd never said her name before. She would have remembered. It sounded sinfully sexy on his lips. She found her own dry and licked them before answering. "I talk to a lot of men."

Ten to one, she was referring to men like her car mechanic and her doctor. Chris leaned his elbow on the table and propped up his head, his eyes on her. For the moment his spoon was retired. His curiosity was aroused.

"Do you date? Do you ever go out with any of the applicants?"

"No, never. That would be unethical somehow." She didn't see a point in telling him about the two fiascoes in her life after Patrick died. It would sound incredibly adolescent and he'd only laugh at her. "I don't do dates."

She shrugged carelessly, pushing the subject away. Then, because he was being so genial about it, she found herself confiding in him.

"To be honest, I haven't got the slightest idea what to do on a date. The thought of it makes me freeze up." There, now he probably thought she was some sort of weirdo. "I never really dated, you see."

Amused, Chris looked toward Danny, who was embroiled in an animated conversation with his friend, complete with hand gestures. "Did the three wise men bring the same gifts this time as they did the first?"

She laughed and shook her head. "I already told you, Danny's father and I had known each other since we were children. Four years old is a long way to go back. We were almost always friends and it just progressed from there."

It had been a nice, safe route to pursue. She'd felt a tingle, but there had been no fear in entering into the relationship with Patrick. It was as if it had always been there, just waiting for her, like a special dress hanging in the closet, waiting for her to put it on.

Her reasoning fascinated him. "Yet you run a dating service."

"It's not as strange as it sounds. You don't have to experience it to do it for others. Otherwise, women would never have confidence in male gynecologists, would they?" Now that she was almost full, she had gotten selective about what she was going to eat. She turned the platter around until she could get at the mint chip more easily. "I think people are happier in pairs, as long as it's the right pair. The reams of personal ads point to that."

Rosemary was surprised when he took a bit of the mint himself. Their tastes ran along the same lines, she thought. Either that, or he just didn't want to reach over for some of the cookies and cream. "I just try to help them along and pay my bills as I do it."

He wanted to keep her talking. "Does it pay the bills, if you don't mind my asking?"

Teri had warned her that she was too open, but there didn't seem to be any harm in telling Chris what he wanted to know.

"No, I don't mind you asking, and yes, finally, it does. It took a few years to get established, but now we're holding our own." A satisfied smile curved her mouth. "I get a lot of word-of-mouth business."

He found himself growing more intrigued with her by the moment. This wasn't a game she was playing with him. She was serious. "But you still don't date?"

She shook her head. "No, I don't date."

He still thought that was rather unusual. "Why? You're an attractive woman . . ."

She didn't want to get into defending herself. "I'm a busy woman and I'd be the first to admit that I would be a lousy date."

He'd had dinner at her house and had been with her at the ice-cream parlor for the past forty-five minutes. Chris saw no basis for her statement.

"Why?"

Rosemary shrugged, wishing Danny would return. She tried to make eye contact, but at this distance it wasn't easy. "Because I'm a dull date."

Was she serious? He grinned. "I don't find you dull."

There was an easy explanation for that. "That's because this isn't a date. We're just sitting here, talking." She gestured toward the door, silently willing Mary Smith to appear. The door remained unopened.

"Waiting for your date to arrive," she concluded on an exasperated note.

Chris shook his head. He didn't bother looking toward the entrance. "I don't think she's coming." He glanced at the big, red-rimmed clock mounted over the long soda counter again just as Danny returned.

"Jeff says hi," Danny told his mother, sliding into his seat opposite them. "Hey, you guys almost finished this thing." He sank his spoon into the gooey mess that was left and began to eat quickly.

Chris looked at Rosemary. "You know, I think I've been stood up."

She hated to admit it, but she thought he was right. He said it so casually, it was almost as if he didn't care. But she knew he had to. Wouldn't anyone, if they were stood up?

She placed her hand on his. "Oh, God, Chris, I am so sorry." She bit her lip. Though he was being blasé about it, she felt guilty for having put him through this. "There's got to be a good reason why she's not here, I'm sure of it. I've had the business for over four years and I've never had a no-show before."

He laughed. "That makes two of us."

She was certain of that. No woman in her right mind would have ever stood him up.

Danny stopped eating long enough to grin broadly at them. "Lucky thing for Chris that we came here, huh, Mom?"

She thought that having them here had probably intensified the sting of being stood up rather than muted it. But before she could respond, Chris answered.

"He's right. At least this way it wasn't a waste of my time." He smiled at her. "I'm having a good time. And the ice cream is excellent."

She was embarrassed for him and mortified that she had inadvertently been the cause of it. "I just don't know what to say." She realized that her hand was still on his and withdrew it, dropping it into her lap.

"Then don't say anything. Just help me eat this before it melts all over the place." His spoon hit against Danny's and they both laughed. Chris slanted Rosemary a look. "It's not your fault," he said softly.

She felt herself melting faster than the ice cream.

Chris placed his spoon down temporarily and picked up his napkin, then leaned toward her.

"You've got some pistachio right here." Rather than hand her the napkin, he dabbed it at the corner of her mouth.

The air stopped in her lungs. The look in his eyes told her that he had an entirely different method of cleanup in mind. But this was a public place and they were with her son, so he had to curtail his impulses.

It was all there for her to see.

With effort, Rosemary swallowed the huge lump obstructing her throat.

"Thank you." Very slowly, she took the napkin from him and wiped her mouth. "All right?"

"More than all right," he assured her.

She dropped her eyes, not quite knowing what to do with herself. He made her feel wonderful and confused and flustered all at the same time.

Chris looked at the dish. The mounds of ice cream had been demolished and consumed. All that remained of the lofty structure were a few wisps of tired whipped cream and a few wayward nuts.

"I think we've done justice to this offering, how about you?"

Rosemary nodded, throwing in her spoon. "I couldn't fit in another drop of whipped cream even with a shoehorn."

"Now that I'd like to see." Chris laughed and raised his hand for the check.

The waitress saw him and was at their table almost immediately. "Will there be anything else for you?" Pen poised over her pad, she smiled at Chris and Danny, completely ignoring Rosemary.

"No, thanks." His eyes shifted toward Rosemary. *Maybe later.* "I'd like the check, please."

Danny suddenly came to life. "Hey, it's my treat," he protested. He took out a long white envelope from the inside pocket of his jacket. The envelope was sagging from the weight of the change that was in it.

Rosemary's heart swelled.

Her expression was not lost on Chris. He placed his hand on top of Danny's. "Why don't you let me pay, Danny?" His gaze took them both in. "For the pleasure of your company."

Danny considered Chris's offer for a moment. He thought of all the other things that he could buy with his money. Tempted, undecided, Danny took the dilemma to his mother.

"Is it still a Mother's Day present if he pays?"

She nodded. "Absolutely. I always said it was the thought that counted, Danny, not the money."

"Yeah, you did." His head bobbed up and down enthusiastically. "Okay," he told Chris. "I guess I can let you pay." He drew himself up importantly. "But I leave the tip."

Rosemary noted that the waitress looked as if she'd rather have Chris leave the tip, and in something other than currency.

"You're on, Danny." Chris laughed. The waitress handed him the bill and he showed it to the boy. "Can you do fifteen percent of that?"

"Sure I can. I'm in fifth grade. We just covered that." Danny looked to his mother for corroboration.

She nodded. "I checked the homework assignment to prove it."

"Okay." Chris dug into his pocket and took out a ten, then left it on the check, in case Danny's math suddenly failed him. Danny covered the bill with a dollar ten in nickels and dimes.

Chris rose and the waitress shifted only slightly to get out of his way. "Ready?" he asked Rosemary.

She looked at the clock above the counter. It was a little after twelve and there hadn't been a single female with or without a white flower entering in the last hour. Mary Smith wasn't about to show.

Rosemary sighed. This *had* been a failure. Her first. "Ready."

Chris took her arm as she slid out. He toyed with a thought and then decided that he had nothing to lose. "Do you have any other plans for Mother's Day?"

Her own mother lived in Florida and she had already called her this morning. Other than a simple dinner with a cake she had made, there was nothing on her agenda. She looked at Danny, wondering if he had anything else up his sleeve. But the boy shook his head.

"No," she told Chris. "I guess not. Why?" She half expected him to suggest that he come over later and work with the dog.

But he surprised her. "Great. How would you like to drive up to Carmel with me and meet my parents?"

If she had been drinking, she would have choked. "Excuse me?"

He placed a hand to the small of her back and guided her to the door. "Well, it is Mother's Day and I promised my mother that I'd come up later this afternoon—after my date was over," he added significantly. She winced. "I thought that Danny might like to come along with me to see the kennel. And since you shouldn't be alone on Mother's Day—" he exchanged looks with Danny, who nodded "—I thought you might like to join us."

Danny was all for it, his eyes lit like rockets bursting in the sky on the fourth of July. "Can Rocky come with us, too?"

Chris acted as if that was a given. "Sure. There's always room for one more dog."

Rosemary hesitated. She had work to catch up on and she felt as if she was intruding on the special relationship that Danny was forming with Chris.

"I don't know," she said reluctantly. "Why don't you two—"

Danny clutched at her hand. "Please, Mom? It'll be fun and you never get to go anywhere."

Well, that certainly made her look like a stick in the mud. She looked at Chris, flushing. "He makes me sound like Rapunzel."

Chris touched a tendril that hung loose at the nape of her neck. It sent shivers down her spine. "Well, you've got the hair for it."

"I'm short about eighteen feet," she laughed. Her hesitation evaporated. "Okay, if you're sure your mother won't mind."

She obviously didn't know his mother. He was going to take great delight bringing Rosemary to visit. "My mother would love another woman to talk to, even if it's just for the afternoon. It'll give her a chance to complain about the men in her life. Namely my dad and me. She doesn't mean it," he told Danny, "but she does love getting things off her chest once in a while."

Rosemary eyed the door as they walked out and then looked up and down the street, secretly hoping that Mary Smith wasn't hurrying up the block with a very plausible excuse on her lips.

This ripple of excitement she was experiencing was because she was going on an outing that meant a lot to Danny, nothing more. She was just doing this for Danny.

"What does one wear to a puppy farm?" she asked as she got into her car.

"A very patient smile. See you at your place in about an hour," Chris told her as he walked down the block to his own car. He figured that would give her enough time to get ready.

# 6

Rosemary sat back in the passenger seat of Chris's car as he drove them home from Carmel. Darkness hugged the road, broken by an occasional beam of light from an oncoming car. They were coming with more frequency, cutting through the dark like light sabers in the night, now that they were almost at their destination.

All in all, it had been a rather incredible day. She'd actually spied on one of her clients—there was absolutely no other way she could describe what she had done by going to the restaurant where Chris was to meet his potential date. Then she'd spent a very pleasant and stimulating hour gaining approximately five pounds.

After that she'd been whisked away to Carmel for the remainder of the day. She wasn't the type to just "whisk" anywhere anymore. For the longest time now, everything about her life had been organized. It followed a natural order, a schedule, steps that were imprinted on her brain if not on a page. She'd been a spontaneous person once, but that had been lost in the scramble to make a living and simultaneously raise a boy single-handedly.

To top the day off, she'd been completely overwhelmed by a litter of new puppies, all of which wanted the laces off her sneakers in the worst way.

She glanced at Chris as the headlights from another oncoming car dramatically outlined his chiseled profile. He looked a lot like his father, she thought. Except for his eyes and his mouth. Both were soft, sensual, and almost alluringly wicked. Those he had gotten from his mother.

Melissa Maverick looked young enough to pass for Chris's sister rather than the matronly mother Rosemary had envisioned on the way up to the kennel. Young in her looks and her attitude.

Both of Chris's parents had welcomed her and Danny as if they had always been coming up there for visits instead of just being someone Chris had whimsically decided to drop into their midst.

Melissa had instantly taken charge of Danny, reminiscing about Chris when he had been that age. Everyone but Chris had gotten a kick out of the detour she had taken down memory lane.

Rosemary smiled, thinking of the conversation at the dinner table. It had been a long time since she'd felt that comfortable anywhere. She glanced at Chris. "I think your parents are very nice."

He was pleased at the comment. There had been a rather wild, undisciplined period in his life, but now that he was older and had worked it out of his system, he saw his parents for what they were. Decent, loving people who had tried to do their best in raising him.

"Yeah, I like them." His mouth quirked in an amused expression. "Took a bit of doing, raising them, but I think they turned out all right."

His words struck a familiar chord. She grinned. How many times, while she had been growing up, had she felt the same way about her own parents? That she was raising them instead of the other way around?

"I guess all kids feel that way, that they had a hand in forming their parents." She wondered if that went through Danny's mind, as well. Probably.

"Well, actually, they do." Chris glanced at her and saw the puzzled look on her face. She probably thought he was putting her on. "A kid has a way of turning you into a more responsible person. And making you remember what it was like to be a kid at the same time. The world through a kid's eyes is really terrific. I'd forgotten about that world until Danny started hanging around with me." He smiled fondly. He honestly enjoyed being with the boy. It made him seriously think about having children of his own. "There's a great deal of joy in that kid."

Yes, she knew. Danny certainly had brought a lot into hers. "And energy. Don't forget energy."

Chris glanced in his rearview mirror at the occupants in his back seat. He grinned. "Sure doesn't look that way now."

Rosemary looked over her shoulder. Danny was slumped over in the corner of the car, fast asleep. His arm dangled around Rocky's neck. The puppy was dozing with her muzzle splayed on his thigh.

She wished she had thought to bring a camera with her. This was one of those keeper moments you pasted into family albums. She lingered a moment, her chin resting against the seat, imprinting it on her heart.

She turned around in her seat. "The way he was going today, I didn't think anything would tire him out." But then, so what else was new? "Danny's always running everywhere instead of walking."

That didn't sound so unusual to Chris. It sounded wonderfully normal. He switched lanes, easing to the right for his exit. "Maybe Danny's just excited about living."

Rosemary smiled. She liked the sound of that. "Maybe."

Chris took the off ramp on Culver. The light at the end of the street was red. He eased his foot onto the brake, coming to a full stop. There was no impatient desire to get home tonight. He was enjoying her company too much.

"What about you? What would make you excited about living?" he asked.

She couldn't help wondering what he thought of her, though she assured herself it was only idle curiosity, nothing more. "I am excited about living. I just show it in my own fashion." She smiled. "Call it quiet excitement."

He spared her a look before turning back to the long winding road. It was such a nice night, he decided to take the back streets of Bedford to reach home. Quiet excitement. The term seemed to suit her.

"Yeah, I guess maybe you have something there at that."

The atmosphere was pregnant with things that weren't being said. Things that she didn't want said. If they were, it would place an entirely different spin on the day.

Suddenly needing an ally, something to break up the mood, Rosemary leaned over and switched on the radio. When the digital light blinked on, she saw that Chris had it set to his station. It was only natural. Somehow that was soothing.

She'd tuned in in the middle of a song. A singer was threatening a male suitor with the eminent return of her boyfriend who was going to make him sorry he was ever born. Rosemary sat back and let the tension ease away from her body.

*Friends, we're just friends, nothing more. Nothing to get nervous about.*

Looking at the station's call numbers, Rosemary suddenly realized what time it was. She straightened as she shifted toward him. "Isn't this a little late for you to be up?"

Chris looked at the digital readout on his dashboard. He didn't quite catch her drift, but played along. "It's five to eleven. We've got a full hour left before the footman turns into a mouse."

"No, I meant your radio program—"Roamin' With The Maverick." You're on from five to nine, aren't you?" He nodded. "Well, don't you usually go into the station an hour before you're on?"

Danny had to have told her that. Chris wondered if she had asked, or if the boy had volunteered the information. "Yes."

She glanced at the clock as if for reinforcement. "By the time we get home, that gives you—what?—four hours to sleep if you fall asleep on your doorknob."

The image made him laugh. The question made him smile. "Worried about me, Rosemary?"

She shrugged and fixed her eyes on the road. "It comes naturally with being friends."

He remembered what she had told him about Patrick. The thought pleased him. They were taking baby steps, but they were steps. "Then we're friends?"

"Yes." She would have thought that was self-evident. She wouldn't have let someone she disliked interact with her son. Didn't he realize that?

He nodded and smiled as he turned down another road. "Good."

"I wouldn't have gone up to Carmel with you if we weren't." Rosemary didn't know why, but she felt compelled to explain that to him. Or maybe she just wanted to put things into perspective. For herself as well as for Chris.

Chris smiled. Was she aware that there was a nervous edge to her voice? The one that always seemed to creep in whenever he got a little too close?

"All right, friend, since you're worried, rest easy. I'm not going in tomorrow. I put in for a vacation day. Actually, I thought I'd be sleeping over at my parents' house tonight." This, however, had turned out a whole lot better.

So he had already made plans before he'd asked them to come along. "Why didn't you?"

The path to their development was lined with huge, towering trees on both sides. Aging eucalyptus trees, their scaly barks hidden in the darkness, nodded shaggy heads at them as they drove by. It made for a very tranquilizing atmosphere.

It offset the charge Chris felt within.

"Because tomorrow's Monday and Danny has to go to school."

That he was so accommodating was sweet, but she hadn't wanted to interfere with his plans. "But we didn't have to come up with you."

She still didn't get it, did she? But she would. In time. "Yeah, you did." Chris turned down the radio so that the music was only a whispered backdrop. He'd rather listen to the sound of her voice. "I had a feeling you needed some spontaneity in your life."

Rosemary frowned. Somehow, she didn't want him to think of her as a stick in the mud, though she knew it didn't really matter. Friends were supposed to like you no matter what you were.

"It's the Rapunzel thing again, isn't it?"

He glanced at her hair. It had long since come tumbling down after one puppy jumped at her with such enthusiasm he'd knocked her over. Pins had gone flying all over the place and they had all had to scramble quickly to retrieve them before the puppies made a snack out of them.

"In part," he agreed. "And maybe I just wanted the company on the drive there. Danny certainly enjoyed the puppies."

There was no contesting that. Rosemary laughed as she summoned an image of her son on the ground, surrounded by enthusiastic pink tongues.

"I don't think he has to wash his face for at least a week. As a matter of fact, I'm surprised he has a face left."

"They can get pretty enthusiastic." Chris looked down at her feet. There was a small hole in the toe of her left sneaker. "Sorry about your shoes."

In reply, she wiggled her foot. A toe was sticking out of the hole. "Don't give it another thought. It made the puppies happy." Her eyes shone as she talked. "Besides, to carry one of your metaphors further, Cinderella did come back from the ball without one of her shoes."

Chris made a right turn onto a road of orange groves doomed to extinction. Progress was everywhere and sometimes he wondered if it was such a good thing. There would be a brand-new shining development there next spring instead of aged orange trees. He would have preferred the trees.

Their development was just up ahead. He made another right and entered it. The streets all fed into one another like a well-fitting puzzle. He knew the way back with his eyes shut. "I'd hardly call a trip to a kennel going to the ball."

She wondered if he was making fun of her, then decided that he wouldn't do that. It was one of the things she liked about him. With his looks and his popularity, he still wasn't egotistical or sarcastic. He could have easily been both.

"Different strokes for different folks."

Chris came to a stop in her driveway. Turning off the ignition, he hooked an arm over the side of the seat and looked at her. "And you certainly are different, Rosemary."

Why did she suddenly smell his cologne? And why did it feel so closed-in here?

"Good different or bad different?" God, she couldn't believe she was actually asking that. It was a flirtatious question that had no place between them.

His mouth curved, the smile rising. "Unique different."

She laughed. "Nice save. Well, thanks for an extraordinary day."

He seemed to draw closer without moving a muscle. "It doesn't have to be over."

Something trembled within her, something small and fearful. And excited. Rosemary felt as if she'd just lost her footing on the ice. Any minute now her feet were going to fly out from underneath her as she struggled for balance.

"Yes, it does. I have a son to get to bed, a puppy to cage and..."

Her mind went blank as her voice just faded away.

Chris leaned over, just as she knew he would, and touched his lips to hers. Why she didn't pull back when there were flares going off in her head spelling Mayday in big, bold letters, was totally beyond her. But she didn't pull back. She just sat there as if every limb in her body had been dismantled and watched his mouth lower to hers.

And then she wasn't watching anymore.

She was experiencing.

Rosemary felt as if she had just slid off the ice floe completely. Except that it wasn't ice anymore. It was the top of a waterfall and she was plummeting downward at an amazing speed.

So fast that her breath had been sucked out of her lungs.

She wanted to curl her arms around his neck. She wanted to fall into the kiss. But something inside her was afraid. So very afraid.

Of what, she didn't know. Herself. Feelings. The unknown. Being hurt. All of the above.

It held her back.

It was so much easier dealing with other people's lives, when she could keep a clear head and keep herself emotionally divorced from what was happening.

She couldn't begin to deal with this.

Her lips were sweeter than anything he had ever tasted. Tempting, ripe. Giving. He felt her hesitation at the same time that he felt the passion bridled just within.

She was exciting and exhilarating and he wanted to go on kissing her like this all night. Forever.

Alarms and common sense were rushing to her rescue. Rosemary wedged her hands against Chris's chest as if she were trying to pry herself away instead of push him back. With effort, she succeeded.

She was breathless and stunned. Her head felt like an apple tumbling out of a fruit bin and rolling along the floor.

"I really have to go," she whispered.

No, she didn't. And he didn't want her to. "Rosemary—"

The alarms were growing louder. She wasn't supposed to be doing this. She had fixed him up with someone else. Granted that the woman hadn't come, but there still might be a good reason for that. Besides, she didn't kiss, didn't date. She didn't need to. She was happy with her life. Happy, happy, happy.

Her eyes implored him. "Please. As my friend. Understand."

He wanted to find out exactly what it was that he was supposed to understand, but the note of distress in her voice had him backing away. For now.

"Fine," he said casually, though he felt anything but fine.

Unhooking her seat belt, Rosemary was out of the car as if she had been ejected by a spring. She quickly opened the rear door and leaned in. Rocky, awake, whimpered in protest as she was moved from Danny's lap.

Chris rounded the trunk. "Here, let me carry Danny in for you. He's too heavy."

She was about to wake Danny up and walk him into the house and up to his room, the way she did on the rare occasions when he fell asleep on the floor in front of the television set.

Rosemary looked at Chris over her shoulder. "I can manage."

Despite her protest, Chris moved her out of the way. "Yes, I know, you told me all about managing. Now let me tell you all about stubborn." He fixed her with a knowing look. "You're being it. Now stay out of the way." She opened her mouth to protest. "As a friend."

She pursed her lips together, but the smile came anyway.

"Okay. Thanks." Rosemary waited until Chris had Danny in his arms, then she picked up the puppy and followed in Chris's wake. Juggling the dog to one side, thinking that she was already growing too large to be handled this way, Rosemary pulled her key out of her pocket and opened the front door.

"Where's his room?" Chris headed toward the stairs even as he asked. Since the house had the same layout as his, he had a pretty good idea which room Danny had chosen as his. The one with the window seat.

"Upstairs." Rosemary pointed needlessly. "First one you come to." She headed to the family room where Chris had set up Rocky's cage. "I'll just put Rocky away and join you there."

The door to the enclosure that Rocky thought of as her home within a home was standing open. Kneeling, Rosemary slid the puppy into her cage with a minimum of effort. The dog plopped down, one ear dipping into the empty dog dish. It was her favorite sleeping position.

"You're growing up too fast, dog," Rosemary murmured, rising to her feet. "And so's your master. I guess I'm just going to have to get used to it."

She heard a floorboard creak over her head. Chris. Rosemary hurried upstairs to Danny's room.

Chris had placed the boy on his bed and had already removed his shoes and socks. He was just throwing a sheet over Danny when she entered.

Chris looked up. "I thought you might just want to let him sleep."

She nodded. She didn't want to disturb Danny. His sleep was more important than being properly dressed for it. "We seem to be on the same wavelength."

Chris's eyes met hers and held for a long moment. "Maybe." He slid his hands into his back pockets. "Well, I guess I'd better call it a night myself."

For a moment Rosemary considered offering Chris something. A cool drink or a late snack. But she decided against it. It was better if he left now. She didn't want to give him the wrong idea.

*Which is what?* a small voice inside her head inquired.

The trouble was, she didn't know anymore. Everything was getting so muddled. If he hadn't kissed her, it would have been a little simpler for her to sort out. Not much, maybe, but at least a little.

Chris left the room. Rosemary hurried after him down the stairs. She stopped at the front door. "Danny really had a wonderful time. Thanks."

"Sure thing." He touched her face lightly with his hand. He felt excitement telegraph through him. If they were on the same wavelength, then she would have felt it, too. "Maybe we can do it again sometime." Chris saw the uncertainty enter her eyes again. He glanced toward the puppy cage, where Rocky was stretched out on her side, sleeping. "Just the four of us."

There was safety in numbers. With Danny along, she could be Danny's mother. Rocky's keeper. Chris's friend. It wouldn't be a one-on-one situation with the spotlight on her "one."

She smiled at him. "That sounds good to me."

Yes, she was certainly a unique woman, he thought. The signals he was receiving were very, very mixed. He tried to concentrate on what he had felt when they'd kissed. What he had read in her kiss.

Chris turned just before he left and ran a thumb along her lower lip. He wanted to kiss her again, badly, but knew he couldn't press. He'd just have to wait a little longer.

He had the satisfaction of seeing a flicker of desire flower in her eyes. *Yeah, me, too.*

"'Night, Rosemary."

"'Night."

Rosemary closed the door and then leaned against it, feeling suddenly, utterly boneless.

"Oh, boy," she murmured with a sigh. "Oh, boy, oh, boy, oh, boy."


"So this woman actually didn't show?" Teri looked properly shocked after Rosemary had filled her in on Mary Smith's glaring nonappearance.

Rosemary still felt very guilty about the incident. After all, she had roped Chris into it. "No."

Teri slid open an envelope, shaking her head. "Incredible. And you were there with Danny to see all this not happen?"

"Yes." She started to key in an application, but her mind wasn't on it. It was where it had no business being. On Chris. "Danny insisted on going there for Mother's Day. I didn't have the heart to turn him down." Rosemary didn't realize that Teri had stopped working and was watching her with a great deal more interest than she was giving to her work. "We all wound up sharing one of those monster ice-cream dishes."

There was an intrigued, hopeful look on Teri's face. "And?"

Rosemary attempted to concentrate on what she was typing. The man who had filled out the form had an affinity for cacti. Hadn't she come across that lately?

"And he took us up to his parents' house. They own a kennel and Danny was completely engulfed by puppies." She hit the computer, seeking a match.

Teri studied her face. "How about you? What were you engulfed by?"

Bingo, Rosemary thought as a name appeared on the screen. She pulled up the file and smiled as she skimmed over the particulars. It looked like a good match in the making.

"Puppies," Rosemary answered absently.

Teri looked at her in disgust. "That's all?"

Rosemary looked up from the screen. "What are you getting at?"

What did Rosemary need, a road map? "I just thought that, well, a guy doesn't take a woman to meet his parents every day . . ."

Leave it to Teri to hear only what she wanted to hear. "It wasn't every day. It was Mother's Day," Rosemary stated patiently. "And he was going up to see her. He just asked us to come along since we didn't have any plans."

She hit the print button and waited for the printer to give her a hard copy of the file she'd pulled up. Unless she missed her guess, Tom Kelly was going to really hit it off with Gloria O'Hara. She hoped all the couples who had been paired off and announced on

K-LAS had fared well. Better, at least, than Chris Maverick and his no-show.

She was dealing with a babe in the woods, Teri thought. She planted herself in front of Rosemary's face. "And you believe that?"

Rosemary collected her printed sheet and placed it alongside the application she had been keying in. "Why shouldn't I?"

Exasperated, Teri tried again. "He didn't seem the slightest bit interested in you?"

Rosemary shrugged, suddenly pulled into the conversation. "Well, he kissed me—"

"Hallelujah." Teri clapped her hands together like a member of a revival meeting. "Now we're getting to the good part."

If Teri was bracing herself for "the good part," she was going to be sorely disappointed. "That's it. He kissed me and then he went home."

Rosemary had to have skipped something. "That doesn't sound right."

When was Teri going to get it through her head that she wasn't looking for a romance? "That sounds just the way I want it to sound, Teri." Rosemary frowned. "Except for the kiss part."

Teri looked positively crushed, as if a daydream had just died. "You didn't like it?"

Her cousin's eyes were going to fall out of her head, Rosemary thought. "I didn't say that."

Teri threw her hands up. "Then what the hell are you saying, Rosemary?"

Enough was enough. "That I'm tired of this conversation and we have work to do. That Mary Smith ruined my record by not showing up and it's going to take me a long time to get over that."

Talk about being thickheaded! "I think she did you a favor and you just don't know it."

Rosemary sighed and pointed to the piles of letters that were still stacked in front of Teri, waiting to be opened. "Just get to work, okay? Or I'm going to have to find another assistant."

The letter opener remained immobile next to Teri. "Another brain is more like it. If that golden-voiced hunk in tight jeans kissed me, I sure wouldn't have sent him home with his tail between his legs."

Rosemary picked up another form she had reviewed and began typing that in. "He doesn't have a tail, and if he did it wouldn't have been between his legs—"

The smile on Teri's face was almost lecherous. "Where would you have put it?"

She pointed her finger dramatically at the letters. "Just work."

Teri regarded her cousin thoughtfully. "I guess I'll just have to."

Rosemary continued typing the information from the form into the program without looking at Teri. She missed the glint in Teri's eyes. "Good idea."

Teri sighed and she began slicing the letters open again. "Yeah."

# 7

Rosemary looked out the back window. The puppy, exhausted from chasing butterflies all morning that refused to be caught, was stretched out, sleeping on the patio. No doubt saving up energy for when Danny came home from school.

A sixties song was playing in the background. She'd set the dial on K-LAS about six months ago when she had discovered it while flipping stations, and had left it there. The disc jockey who followed Chris was on, making a pitch for a high-priced car.

That meant Chris would be home soon.

"Hey, Rosie, look at this letter." Teri waved it at her to get her attention. "It's from your no-show." She took another look at it. "Or rather, it's from her son. Take a look."

Rosemary's first inclination was to tell Teri to put the letter somewhere and then disregard it. Since the ad campaign, Soulmates, Inc., had been inundated with requests for forms. Someone on the local newspaper had heard the ad and decided to write a piece on personalized dating, featuring Rosemary. Now they were receiving all kinds of letters and telephone calls.

She felt overwhelmed and swamped. And very triumphant. It was all mixed together.

It was kind of, she mused, the way she had felt when Chris had kissed her.

When Rosemary didn't reach for the letter, Teri looked at her in surprise. "Don't you want to see it?" she prodded.

"Oh, all right." Rosemary put her hand out. "Let me take a look at it." Teri leaned over the desk and extended the letter to her. Rosemary settled back, looking at the mailbag Teri had brought in with her. It was completely full. "You know, if things keep up like this, you're going to have to go full-time."

The timing couldn't have been better. Teri grinned as she took a sip of her coffee.

"Fine with me. The kids will be in school for another two months. After that, I'll just bring them along with me."

Rosemary could just picture that. Teri's twins were as rambunctious as the puppy. She was going to have to remember to stock up on herbal tea.

Rosemary glanced at the dormant dog on the patio. Rocky couldn't be referred to as a puppy much longer. In the three days since Mother's Day, the dog seemed to have grown three inches.

Funny how she kept using Mother's Day as her reference point. It seemed as if the world had completely turned around that day. Since he had kissed her. She hadn't been kissed like that, like she was a desirable woman, since Patrick had died.

She had almost forgotten what it had felt like. Wonderful.

*Enough of this. You've got to get your mind back on your work.*

She scanned the letter that Teri had handed her. It was from Tommy, all right, and it was as heartfelt an apology as she had ever seen on paper. She bit her lower lip as she read. Tommy had started throwing up at the last minute, just before Mary was going to leave him with a sitter. Mary did what any mother would do in that kind of a situation. She had taken him to a walk-in clinic.

> She didn't want to write to you about it because she feels funny and embarrassed. I know she wants another chance. She said so, but she's really shy and says maybe it's forthe best. I don't think so. Can you help?
>
> Your friend,
>
> Tommy Smith

*Can I help? Of course I can help,* Rosemary thought, folding the letter and placing it on the desk. Shy, huh? Well, heaven knew she could certainly relate to that. Since Tommy was certain that his mother was just having trouble coming out of her shell, maybe what she needed was a little push.

Mary Smith deserved a chance at happiness and shouldn't be allowed to get in her own way.

Rosemary glanced at the salutation at the top of the letter. Rosemary sincerely wished that the woman had something other than a P.O. box to write to. Why didn't they have a regular address? Were they new here? Transient? Did they live in a motel or a trailer park? And why would that even matter?

Worse yet, there was no telephone number on file to use. Mary could call them, but they couldn't call her. It made things difficult. But not impossible.

Teri decided that she had been patient enough. "What do you think? Shall we give her another chance with the hunk-of-the-month?"

Teri's interest was atypical. Her cousin usually found something to amuse her in the forms. She didn't take Soulmates as seriously as Rosemary did.

"You seem awfully anxious about this match all of a sudden. I thought you were trying to thrust me into Chris's arms."

"And manly arms they are." Teri sighed audibly. "But you weren't thrustable, and I do so hate to see something that delicious wasted." Teri fluttered her dark lashes prettily as she struck a pose.

Rosemary laughed as she shook her head. "You're hopeless."

A little of Teri's amused expression abated, to be replaced by a canny one. "In this room, I'm only number two."

Rosemary raised a brow. She might have known. "Same old song?"

Teri shrugged innocently as she resumed opening letters. "Hey, I'm only humming."

Yeah, right. It wasn't bad enough that Chris was dwelling on her mind. Teri had to keep reinforcing that haunting image at every opportunity. It just wasn't right to date someone she had set up with a client. And besides, she didn't date, she insisted, all but mentally shouting.

"Well, hum something else." Rosemary stared at the letter. There was something here that spoke to her. A crying need written between the lines that was going unanswered. Tommy needed a dad and Mary certainly needed to have a fire lit under her before she would move.

From what she knew, Chris Maverick was just the man to do it. She had to set them up on another date right away.

Even as the thought hit her Rosemary felt a reluctance to act on her impulse. But it was the only way, she told herself. If Chris was with someone else, she wouldn't be having these impossible thoughts about him.

And they *were* impossible. She knew exactly what would happen if she disregarded her principles and went out with him. What would happen would be a big, fat zero and then he'd think of her as a dud. Though it wasn't supposed to make a difference what he thought, Rosemary really didn't want Chris to feel that way about her. And it would happen. She'd bet any amount of money on it.

"Always leave them wanting more" took on a whole new meaning for her.

Teri could see that Rosemary was wrestling with something. She waited a moment before asking. "So how do you figure you'll do it?" Rosemary raised her eyes to her questioningly. "Make Chris say yes again," Teri elaborated.

It really shouldn't be all *that* difficult. "He wasn't exactly furious when she didn't show up." Rosemary smiled without realizing it. "He's not one of those people with an ego to nurture."

"Stop." Teri held up a hand like a patrolman directing traffic. "You're making me salivate." An impish smile curved her mouth. "Just go do what you have to do. I'll man the phones and hold down the fort until you get back."

But Rosemary remained where she was, debating with herself. She wasn't quite as eager as she had originally been to fix Chris up. All the right reasons were there, but her emotions were holding her back.

*You can't have it both ways,* Rosemary insisted silently.

She shrugged, curling the edge of a form between her thumb and forefinger. "I could just wait until he comes over to see Danny and work with Rocky."

Some orchestration was definitely required here. "I'd rather he came over to see Danny and work with you." Teri saw the way Rosemary's brows drew together and she threw up her hands in surrender. "All right, all right, I'll stop."

"Thank you." Rosemary glanced at her watch. It was already an hour past the time that Chris usually arrived. She found herself listening for the sound of his car pulling up in his driveway these days...

Like a puppy waiting for its master to come home, she upbraided herself.

All the upbraiding in the world didn't prevent her from wondering why Chris was late today. He normally returned home like clockwork. Maybe there was someone he was seeing at the station. Maybe—

Maybe it was none of her business. After all, she wasn't involved, except in the most professional of capacities.

And didn't that sound just peachy? she mused sarcastically. It made her sound like one of those ladies of the evening who littered the downtown area of every major city.

Teri looked at her impatiently. "So, you going to sit there, or what?"

"I'm sitting," Rosemary answered brightly. "The 'or what' isn't home yet."

Teri looked at her knowingly. "Listening for him, are we?"

Oh, what was the use? Teri seemed to be determined to throw her together with Chris, via jealousy or any weapon she had. Why couldn't her cousin just leave well enough alone?

"I don't know about you, but I'm not. I just—" The telephone mercifully chose that moment to ring. Rosemary looked at Teri pointedly. "Get that, will you, and do something useful with that mouth of yours."

She felt herself on the edge of exasperation and she never got that way. With anyone. It just proved how strung out she had felt—since Mother's Day.

There was that point of reference again.

Teri laid a hand across her forehead and sighed dramatically. "I just don't know why I take this abuse. Must be the Samaritan in me."

"More like the meddler in you." She pointed toward the wall phone. "Phone?"

Teri rose and picked up the receiver. "Hello, Soulmates, Inc. How may I help you?"

Maybe she could get some work done now, Rosemary thought. The doorbell chimed, playing notes from "Since I Don't Have You."

And then again, maybe not. She sighed as she rose, feeling as if things were slipping right out of her grasp. What was going on? She used to be so organized. How had things gotten so out of hand in three days?

They weren't out of hand, she insisted. At least not much. They'd just gotten a little tangled. All because a hunk in tight jeans had kissed her. And here she was, attempting to give him away.

The doorbell rang again before she could reach it. "I'm coming, I'm coming," she called.

Rosemary pulled the front door open and her heart skipped. *Stupid, stupid, stupid,* she admonished herself as she looked up at Chris. She was a grown woman. This was a ridiculous way to react.

The truth slid from her tongue before she could think to stop it. "Hi, I was just thinking about you."

It was a cool May morning that instantly warmed as he smiled at her. "Anything good?"

She jumped into the heart of the matter, thinking it best. If she let herself bask in that smile, who knew where this would lead? "Well, I have this letter."

He groaned even though his smile remained. "Not another client."

"No." Rosemary motioned Chris in and closed the door behind him. "Not another one. The same one." She watched him for signs of annoyance and was pleased when there weren't any. "I just received another letter from her son in today's mail."

He looked at her. "Danny?"

That was an odd mistake for him to make. "No, Tommy. Her son's name is Tommy," she reminded him. Or had she forgotten to tell him that? She didn't think so, but she wouldn't place bets on anything lately.

Rosemary noticed that Chris was holding a bag and wondered what was in it. Since he didn't mention it, she curbed her curiosity. There were more important things to get to.

"Anyway, Tommy says he was sick on Mother's Day. Mary had to take care of him." It all sounded perfectly plausible to her, if maybe a bit contrived.

Chris looked dubious. "She could have called the Soda Shoppe."

Rosemary looked chagrined. She'd been so eager to absolve Mary, she'd overlooked that. "That's right, she could have. Maybe she was just too worried about her son to think of it."

She could remember several times when Danny had been horribly ill and she had been beside herself with worry. She'd let a great many things slide then.

"Maybe," he agreed. But he hadn't come over to discuss an elusive date who hadn't materialized. He was here for another reason. "Rosemary—"

He had a look in his eyes that she wasn't too sure she wanted to explore.

"Anyway," she hurried on as if he hadn't interrupted. "I'd like to set up another date for the two of you."

He looked at her patiently. "To have another, I would have had to have a first." Studying the intent look on her face, he paused. She was being serious. "And this time she'll show?"

"She'll show." Rosemary made it sound as though she guaranteed it. Why wouldn't the woman show? She was being given a second chance, Rosemary thought. Still, she couldn't help crossing her fingers mentally.

One look at his face told her that she hadn't really convinced him.

"Say, why don't you take her to that classic film showing you mentioned the other day? You know, the one at the university on Friday night? According to her form, she really likes old movies."

*Yes, I know.* "Friday's only two days away. Can you set it up that fast?"

It wouldn't be easy, but she could manage. "I don't see a problem," she said a bit more cheerfully than was necessary. "They don't have a telephone, but—"

Chris looked amused. "Planning on using smoke signals?"

"Very funny. No, a note." He *was* interested. She could tell. Rosemary talked quickly, not wanting to lose the momentum. "The post office box is a local one. I can stop by and drop off the letter myself on my way to pick up Danny at school this afternoon. She'll get it by tomorrow morning." Running out of breath, Rosemary looked at him hopefully. "What do you say?"

"All right, if you're sure she'll come. I guess I can give it another shot." He looked at her. "I don't seem to be seeing anyone right now."

She felt a definite pang at his words. If there hadn't been such an immense wall within her, such a stumbling block, she might have been able to surmount it and get to the other side.

And to Chris.

No, she had to stop thinking like that. She was setting him up with a very nice woman who seemed to be his perfect match in every way except punctuality. It would all work out to everyone's satisfaction.

Well, maybe not to everyone's, but she wasn't going to think about that.

Rosemary saw an action figure Danny had forgotten lying under the coffee table. She bent down and picked it up, placing it on top. That was all she needed, for the puppy to swallow a toy and have to be rushed off to the vet at some ungodly hour.

She realized that Chris was just standing there, his head cocked slightly to the side, studying her. She felt uncomfortable again.

"What?"

The bag's drawstring around his wrist, he pushed his hands into his front pockets. "Something just occurred to me. You do this sort of matchmaking service for money, don't you?"

She had already told him about all that. Why did he think she had advertised on his show? "Yes," she answered cautiously.

"And this Mary Smith isn't paying you." He spoke as if his words were building blocks and he was slowly piling them one on top of another with an end structure in mind.

"No, finding her a match was part of the contest," Rosemary reminded him.

He nodded. "And I'm not paying you."

"No, of course not." She was roping him into this. How could she be asking him for money? What was he getting at?

He knew he was baiting her. But it was fun to tease her. She looked so intense. "Then why are you so determined to set this up?"

That was simple enough, at least for her—no, she amended, at least as far as *he* was concerned. It got a little more complicated for her.

"It's a matter of honor and principle now," she told him. "I like to live up to commitments and I did promise Tommy a date for his mother."

She looked adorable when she was being noble. "Okay, you talked me into it."

Impulsively, she hugged him. She thought it was safe. "You're wonderful."

His arms closed around her and she realized that safe was not a word to use around him just yet. "I keep trying to tell you."

She felt something thud against her back. The bag he had brought with him. Curiosity finally got the better of her. She released her hold on him and stepped back. "What's that?"

He'd almost forgotten. "Oh, I brought you a gift." Chris offered the bag to her.

She looked at the bag. It was from a local shoe store. But he might have just been using it. "You mean for Rocky, don't you?"

He shook his head, offering it to her. "No, I mean for you. It's not so much a gift as a replacement, really."

He really had her curiosity aroused. She took the bag from him and opened it. There was a shoe box inside. Her curiosity growing, she took the box out and then opened it.

Since it was a shoe box in a bag from a local shoe store, she shouldn't have been surprised when she saw shoes in it. But she was.

He had brought her a pair of very stylish athletic shoes. They were too fancy to be called sneakers, like the pair she'd just thrown out.

Rosemary took one out and held it up. "Why?"

He shrugged. "Because one of the puppies ate your sneaker."

Rosemary laughed. Her shoes had to have been at least five years old, if not more. "They were old and tough. The puppy probably had indigestion." She tried to give him the box back. "I can't accept this."

But he wouldn't take it. "Yes, you can." His voice lowered and became incredibly sensual. "It's not as if I brought you lingerie or anything personal. They're for your feet. Running shoes."

They would be completely wasted on her. She didn't use shoes for anything but walking, and besides, she tended toward thrift market bargains, not expensive sports marts. "But I don't run," she protested.

Very carefully, he closed the lid on the box and placed her hands around it. Chris pressed a kiss to her temple. "Yeah, you do. Keep them. It'll assuage my conscience."

The last gift she'd received from a man had been from Patrick. She didn't know how to react. Or if she should even accept them.

"But—"

He arched a brow. "If you give them back, I'm pulling out of the deal."

She had a feeling that he would, too. Rosemary sighed, tucking the box under her arm. "All right, you drive a hard bargain."

Her choice of words made him laugh. "Not yet, but I might."

She wasn't sure what he was talking about, but had a feeling that she should let it go. She held the box up and checked the size on the side. It was the right one. "How did you know my size?"

"I asked Danny."

That didn't answer anything. "And he knew?" Danny didn't even know his *own* shoe size—how had he known hers?

She knew her son, he thought with a grin. "No, he didn't know, but he fished the chewed-up sneaker out of the garbage for me. I took it to the shoe store." He made it sound as if that was a completely normal thing to do.

That must have been a pretty sight. Rosemary could just picture what the salesman had thought, handling a ripe sneaker fresh out of the garbage.

She remembered how annoyed she'd been when she had found the garbage lid off and the trash upset. "And here I thought it was the dog that had made such a mess."

Chris laughed and threaded his arm around her easily as he walked toward the door. "That's why people have dogs, Rosemary. They make wonderful companions and terrific scapegoats. You can blame them for practically everything."

Very carefully, because she liked it too much and didn't want to, Rosemary eased out from beneath his arm. "All right, so it's a date?" She saw the surprised look enter his eyes. "For you and Mary, I mean," she added quickly.

He dug deep for a helping of patience. "I already said yes."

She needed details to tell Mary. "What time does the movie start?"

"Seven." Showings always began at seven o'clock. There were only two shows and he always caught the first one, too tired because of his work schedule to stay up for the second showing.

She tried to recall what he had told her originally. "And it's at the Berkeley theater?" He nodded. "You'll be waiting for her outside." It wasn't exactly a question so much as a hopeful statement.

"I'll be waiting outside," he repeated. "She looks like you, right?"

Rosemary thought of the description on the form, not noticing the way he had looked at her when he asked. It was uncanny that she and Mary were the same height and coloring. And exactly the same age. But then, everyone had at least one twin and she supposed that Mary Smith might be hers.

"Yes, but I'll have her holding a flower, like last time."

"There was no last time," he reminded her.

He had forgotten, she thought. "That's what I told her to be holding when I arranged it. I mean, lots of people look alike and wear the same colors, but how many are going to be holding a white flower?"

He grinned, toying with the earring that she wore. He hit it with the tip of his finger and the hoop swayed to and fro. "I don't know. How many?"

God, he was standing too close to her again. Why did the last five inches around the perimeter of her body always change the situation from pleasant to scary? Deliciously so, but scary nonetheless.

She stilled the earring with her hand. But not the shivers that persisted afterward.

"None." Rosemary looked down at the shoes again and flushed. "You really didn't have to replace them, you know."

"Just say 'thank you, Chris,'" he prompted good-naturedly.

She hugged the box to her as he opened the door and stepped outside. "Thank you, Chris," she parroted.

"See, it wasn't so hard." Impulsively, he dove his fingers into her hair and began to lower his mouth to hers.

Her eyes almost fluttered shut before she came to her senses. Alarms the size of the bell at Notre Dame went off in her head.

"Thank you. See you later." And with that, the door suddenly closed in his face.

"Maybe it's harder than I thought," Chris muttered to himself.

Shoving his hands into his pockets, he walked back to his house. And pondered on his upcoming date with the elusive Mary Smith.

# 8

⟶ ⟵

"No, absolutely not." Rosemary looked at Danny, surprised that he'd even suggest such a thing.

Her protest ricocheted around the kitchen. Teri had left to pick up the twins and go home with them. Rosemary had hoped to work on a few more files, but her concentration had completely shattered when Danny had come up to her and asked if they could go to the same movie theater where Chris was scheduled to meet with Mary Smith.

Talk about déjà vu. This had Mother's Day written all over it.

Rosemary pushed back her chair and got up. The work would keep until after dinner. She could do with a sizable break.

Unwilling to give up so easily, Danny followed her into the living room. Rocky dashed after his heels, ready to play. But at the moment Danny was far more interested in the conversation he was having with his mother than his beloved puppy.

Rosemary began straightening up. Danny tugged on her sleeve for her undivided attention. "But, Mom, what if she doesn't show up again? Then Chris'll be all alone."

Danny was giving voice to exactly the same thoughts that she had been having. What if this Mary person *didn't* show up again? Then this guilty feeling she was carrying around with her would be twice as large.

Rosemary had been convinced that Mary Smith would definitely turn up this time. When she'd returned from a quick errand this morning, there'd even been a call from Mary saying she would be at the theater tonight. Teri had taken the message and given it to her as soon as she'd come in.

But as the hour of the date approached, Rosemary felt herself growing uneasy.

If Chris were stood up again, it would be all her fault. Mary might be the one who didn't show, but she would be the one in the doghouse, so to speak, she thought, glancing at Rocky.

"She'll show, Danny," Rosemary insisted. She sounded far less convinced than she wanted to.

Danny moved his dog to one side. He drew closer to his mother. "But if she doesn't, won't you feel *guilty?*" He said the word with three times as much feeling as he did the others.

Rosemary looked at him sharply. "Thanks, I needed that." She'd never lied to Danny or put him off. Now wasn't the time to start.

"Yes," she admitted, albeit reluctantly. "I probably will, at that." They both knew there was no "probably" about it. She was a pushover when it came to other people's feelings.

Danny spread his hands dramatically, the way he'd seen Teri do. "Well, there you go. If we're there to make him feel better about it, it'll be okay." He thought he saw his mother wavering for a minute. "I know Chris, Mom. He's a nice guy. I can talk to him about Rocky and you can talk to him about that Ronald McDonald guy."

Now he had really gotten her attention. Her eyes narrowed. "Who?"

"In the movie," Danny told her impatiently. "You know, the guy you said liked listening to. The guy with the voice."

"Ronald Coleman?"

Danny nodded in response. "Yeah, him."

Rosemary could only stare at Danny, dumbfounded. Sometimes she mentioned actors from the old movies that she liked. Occasionally she even made Danny watch old movies on tape or on one of the cable channels in an attempt to expose him to something a little broader than Saturday morning heroes.

But she hadn't really thought that any of it had sunk in.

Apparently so.

The movie playing at the college theater was *A Tale of Two Cities.* Prompted by curiosity, she had found it listed in the entertainment section of the paper. But what was Danny's reason for looking?

"How do you know what's playing in the movie?"

For just a moment Danny looked flustered, then he shrugged in that careless, little boy fashion he had when things really didn't concern him. "Chris told me yesterday, while we were working with Rocky. He said it was one of his favorites."

Something else they had in common, she thought.

Struggling, she tried to keep her mind on straightening the room. It seemed that the house *always* needed straightening. She supposed if it didn't, she'd be living alone and miserable. Neat, but miserable. It had its compensations.

Danny was shifting from foot to foot, as if he thought the debate was still alive and he had a chance of winning it.

"Well, then he won't mind being alone," she said firmly.

Danny opened his mouth and then shut it again. He actually looked stumped for a minute. But only for a minute. "Um, I thought that since you like this Ronald guy and Chris likes him—"

She tossed the decorative pillow back where it belonged on the sofa. "Wait a minute. Chris likes him, too?"

Danny's head bobbed up and down so hard it seemed as if it weren't really connected to his neck. "Uh-huh. That's what he said." He brightened, knowing he was on the right trail. "Anyway, since you both like him, I thought that maybe I should see him, too."

*Nice try.* She picked up the other cushion, fluffing it. Maybe she could try applying rubber cement to keep the pillows in place. "You have." She tucked it into place. "I made you watch *Lost Horizon*, remember?" She'd all but tied him down. She'd given up after an hour. He just wasn't interested.

Danny looked at her solemnly. "No, I don't remember."

She turned to face him. "Sure you do, it was when..." Her voice trailed off as temptation began to erode her resistance.

This was really against her better judgment. But she had to admit that she *was* curious about the woman who sounded so much like her. And she really did love *A Tale of Two Cities.* Seeing it on the wide screen would be a treat. It had been a long time between treats.

Rosemary pressed her lips together, debating with herself.

Danny knew he was winning. His eyes fairly danced. "Can we go? Can we, Mom? Can we?"

At any moment she expected him to start jumping up and down, the way Rocky did when he offered her a treat. He looked so cute, she felt herself weakening completely. "It'll end past your bedtime."

He was prepared for that one. "It's not a school night. Today's Friday. I can get extra sleep in the morning."

She eyed the dog, who was sitting with her bottom planted on the floor, wagging her tail. It thumped in rhythm against the rug.

"You have to let Rocky out in the morning. That was the deal. And then feed her." Though she was tempted to let him sleep in, Rosemary knew that giving him responsibility was important in the long run. She just had to remain strong about it and not let her natural tendency to take over overwhelm them both.

He wasn't about to protest or argue. She might change her mind if he did. "Right. I'll let her out, feed her and then get more sleep. Please, Mom? Please?"

He looked as if he was going to be crushed if she said no. Oh, well, what would it hurt? "Why does it mean so much to you?"

Like a racehorse in sight of the finish line, he poured everything he had into his answer. "'Cause I want to see this movie you like. And I like Chris. And we haven't been out to see anything in a while. And—"

She held up her hand to stop the flood of words. "Okay, okay. I surrender. We'll go."

Hannibal, completing his journey over the Alps with the elephants, couldn't have looked more happy. "Great, I'll go tell Chris."

He would have flown out the door without touching the ground if she hadn't collared him. Grabbing Danny, Rosemary held him in place. He looked up at her questioningly.

"No, you will not tell Chris. We'll just show up. If he's standing outside, waiting for her, we might say hi. Maybe," she emphasized with a warning. "If we don't see him, we'll assume he's inside with his date. We don't go looking for him, understood?" That would be all she'd need, to have Danny parading up and down the aisles, looking for Chris. Looking like his mother's procurer.

Danny nodded smartly. "Understood." He even saluted her.

Rosemary raised a brow, though she didn't bother hiding the tiny smile that arose. "Don't get wise, Danny."

He looked at her, all innocence. "If I do, it's just because I've got such a wise mom."

She rolled her eyes, then shooed him out the front door. "Go play with your dog—you're covering me in syrup and she might want to lick it off." As he herded Rocky toward the front door, Rosemary glanced at her watch. "If we're going to go, dinner's going to have to be earlier," she warned. Which meant she'd better get started on it soon.

He grinned, one hand on the dog's collar to keep her from running out without him. "No problem. I'm hungry now."

The door banged in his wake as he ran off to do some serious playing. He left behind one very mystified mother.

Ronald Coleman? *A Tale of Two Cities?* Danny? Maybe she should have checked his fingerprints. This just wasn't like her son.

You'd think, Rosemary upbraided herself, that she was the one going on this date with Chris instead of Mary Smith. Butterflies were breeding within her stomach and her palms felt damp.

She was so damn nervous about the woman not showing up.

And yet...

And yet, again, a tiny part of her didn't want the woman to show up at all.

Fine matchmaker she was, hoping one of her matches would fall through. Rosemary shook her head as if to clear it. She had to get a grip.

She wanted this to work, she reminded herself as she parked the car in the small, crowded lot in front of the theater. She wanted Chris to be matched with someone and be happy about it. All she wanted him for was to be a friend. She wanted him to be someone for Danny to talk to, nothing more.

She saw him immediately. The word "more" throbbed in her brain like a recording that had gotten stuck in a groove.

He was standing outside the theater, casually looking around. His thumbs were hooked onto the front loops of his jeans, with his long, artistic fingers extended down, along his tapering hips and flat belly. That same flat belly she had seen sans clothing...

"Mom, you're squeezing my shoulder too hard," Danny protested.

"Sorry." She pulled her hand away. But not her eyes. They were fixed on Chris.

Chris exuded sexuality just by standing and breathing. Chris Maverick looked like an ad, she thought, for everything delectable and desirable.

He was a hot fudge sundae and she was on a diet, she thought firmly.

"There he is, Mom," Danny announced the way one of Columbus's sailors might have cried "Land ho!" after endless days at sea.

She lowered her head slightly and hissed by his ear "Shh, I said—"

Danny pulled his head back and looked at her. "That if he was standing outside the movies, we could go up and say hi."

Why was it that his memory was so selective? "I said *maybe.*"

But Danny's memory refused to be jogged. He curled his hand around his mother's. "Please, Mom? He looks so lonely."

No, that was one thing he didn't look. Not lonely. *He looks so damn sexy, my bones are turning into sawdust.*

And one look around told her that she wasn't the only one who felt that way. She saw several women walking into the theater together. Every single one of them gave Chris the once-over, sizing him up and finding him definitely not wanting.

If anyone was wanting, she thought, it was her.

But wanting and having were two very different things in her book.

*Remember, you turn into a hopeless bore, a klutz, on dates. You want him to think of you that way?*

It was better that he just thought of her as Danny's harried mother.

Rosemary wanted to usher Danny in without Chris noticing, but he was standing so close to the box office, it was impossible.

Even as she approached the entrance, Chris turned his eyes in their direction. The smile that bloomed a moment later was positively lethal.

"Hi!" Danny called. Uncoupling himself from his mother, he rushed up to Chris. Rosemary had no choice but to join them.

"Hi." Chris ruffled Danny's hair, but his eyes were on Rosemary. They made her feel warm. And welcome. And just the least bit disoriented. "No baby-sitting assignment?"

She looked at him, confused.

"You said you had to sit Teri's twins tonight, remember?"

"Oh." She'd forgotten about that excuse. "Teri changed her mind. She and her husband are staying in." Her voice sounded tinny to her ear. "Another awkward moment."

Chris had one arm around Danny's shoulder. Danny looked as pleased as if he had just come first in a race. "Not for me."

She chewed on her lower lip, then, aware of it, she stopped. At this rate she'd get chapped lips. *Saving them for something?* a little voice asked.

"Danny wanted to come."

"I see."

If that wasn't amusement in his eyes, she'd wash her front walk with a toothbrush. She had to make him believe her.

"No, really," she insisted. "He knows I'm crazy about Ronald Coleman and he thought that he should see a movie with Coleman in it."

God, did that sound lame, or what? It had sounded all right when Danny had said it. Out of her mouth, it came out as the world's poorest excuse. He probably thought she was lying.

God, even *she* thought she was lying, and she knew better.

Rosemary cleared her throat and looked around. There was a large enough turnout for the old classic. But none of the women approaching the entrance was carrying a flower of any kind, much less a white one. She had struck out again.

"I take it that she hasn't shown up yet."

He shook his head, exchanging a glance with Danny. "No."

To Rosemary's surprise, Danny maneuvered out from under Chris's arm. He pulled her wrist down and looked at her watch.

"Gee, it's almost seven now. We'd better go in." He looked from Chris to his mother. "We don't want to miss the movie."

The boy was not about to get an Academy Award tonight, she thought. "No, we don't." Rosemary placed her arm around Danny's shoulder and began to usher him toward the box office.

But she wasn't alone.

"I might as well join you." He gave a last perfunctory look around the quad. "It looks as if Mary Smith isn't coming again."

Well, he certainly didn't look upset about it. Not half as upset as she was. For him. For herself, Rosemary had to admit, it was an entirely different matter.

Although it shouldn't be. After all, her reputation was on the line. Chris wasn't the type to spread the word that she had set up a date—no, *two* dates—for him that hadn't materialized, but still, she was taking all this very personally.

Rosemary hesitated a moment. "You don't want to wait any longer?"

"No." He let a couple get ahead of him in line. They were next. "I really hate people who are late."

She could understand that. It was one of her pet peeves. "Yeah, me, too." She saw him opening his wallet. Chris took out a twenty and placed it in front of the cashier.

"Three please."

She fumbled for her own wallet inside the cavern she liked to refer to as her purse. Damn, where was it? "No, you shouldn't have to pay—"

He already had the tickets and was accepting his change. "I want to." He handed Danny a ticket, and then gave one to Rosemary. "I was going to pay for

Mary." His gaze slid from Danny to her. "Why shouldn't I pay for my friends?"

Put that way, she couldn't find it in her heart to refuse. "All right, but I owe you another dinner for this."

He placed an arm around her shoulders and ushered her and Danny inside the theater. "Sounds good to me. Pot roast again?"

One thing she loved to do was cook and she didn't care to repeat herself with guests if she could help it. "I was thinking more in terms of lasagna."

His blue eyes lit up like a small boy's. He wasn't much of a cook himself and he always enjoyed eating good food. "Even better."

He looked at her and she could feel the air sizzling between them, even in the darkened theater. Thank God this wasn't a date or she'd probably turn into a blithering idiot.

There was an easy comfort about being friends.

The movie was wonderful, but that was a given. She'd seen it a total of six times now and loved it more each time she saw it. The company had been equally as wonderful. Several times during the movie Chris had leaned over to her, around Danny who sat between them, and shared a feeling he had about a scene.

She was hard-pressed to remember when she had enjoyed herself more.

Except, perhaps, for last Sunday. And when he'd come over for dinner...

Danny's head had begun nodding somewhere around eight-thirty. He was worn out, no doubt, by his efforts to get her to come here in the first place. A black-and-white movie that crackled with age as well as rich dialogue just didn't hold his interest.

She was secretly grateful to him for goading her into coming.

Danny walked next to her groggily, holding her hand as they left the theater. Chris was holding his other hand to ensure that he didn't stumble. Once outside, they stopped for a moment and sat on one of the benches that hugged the perimeter of the quad.

She looked at Chris as Danny leaned against her shoulder, nodding out. "Did I mention I was sorry?"

"A great deal in the past week."

She shook her head. He was being incredibly nice about this. Someone else would have had her head off by now, venting his embarrassment by proxy.

"I meant about this. About her not showing again." She felt her own anger rising. "I'm going to write to her and give her a piece of my mind. Twice is inexcusable."

"Hey, it turned out all right." He smiled at her and she felt her anger diminishing. "I got to see *A Tale of Two Cities* again." He winked. " 'Tis a far, far better thing I do than I have ever done before.' "

Rosemary was duly impressed. "That sounds just like him."

Chris looked pleased at the compliment. "I practiced a lot in the bathroom as a kid." He didn't often admit that to people. But then, Rosemary wasn't just people.

Chris Maverick really was unusual, she thought. "I can't picture anyone in our generation practicing Ronald Coleman's voice."

"I did." He settled back on the bench, his mouth curving as he remembered. "I did a lot of different voices."

He didn't have to do any imitations to sound good. "You have a nice one of your own."

He laughed just a tad self-consciously. "Thanks."

There were all sorts of things she found herself wanting to know. "So why did you practice voices?"

That was all part of a make-believe world he had occupied. There hadn't been many children to play with where he had grown up. He'd had to be creative. "I thought I was going to be an actor or something like that."

She could just see his face splashed across some magazine cover. Hollywood's newest heartthrob. "What made you change your mind and pick radio?"

"I grew up," he said simply. "And I like the anonymity."

She thought of Teri's comment. "Don't get much of that, I imagine, with your face plastered on the sides of buses."

He shrugged. "I deal with it. It'll pass. They'll be advertising someone else soon enough. And it's not as if I get mobbed, the way I would if I were a successful actor." A june bug buzzed by and he waved it away from Danny. The boy seemed oblivious to the loud noise as he dozed. "I can go to the movies," he continued significantly, "and enjoy myself without having someone jump up and ask for a piece of my shirt."

She laughed. "I can see that happening anyway. You're too good looking for your own good."

*Or mine,* she added silently.

But she was pleased she could talk to him this way. Honestly. It felt comfortable. Right. Just two friends, she thought with relief.

Slightly embarrassed, the way he was whenever his looks came into the conversation, he shrugged away her comment. When he'd been in elementary school, they had referred to him as "Pretty Boy" and he hadn't liked it.

"I always thought my mouth was too soft."

It hadn't felt soft the other night. It had felt firm and wonderful and delicious. And it looked great. "Your mouth is just right."

A smile quirked his lips as a glint entered his eyes. "Really?"

Oops, she'd said the wrong thing again, she thought, even though she'd meant it in exactly the way it had come out. What she hadn't meant was to say it aloud. There was a time for honesty and a time for retreat. She didn't want to spoil the evening by making Chris think that she was coming on to him.

Turning her head, she slanted a look at her son. His head was still resting against her shoulder, but sinking fast. Time to go. She shifted, attempting to rise without throwing Danny off balance.

"I think I'd better get Danny home. He's asleep on his feet."

Chris took hold of Danny's shoulders and brought him to his feet. He looked into the sleepy face. "You okay, Danny?"

"Mumph." The boy barely nodded.

Still holding him up, Chris looked at Rosemary. "Where's your car?"

"Over there, at the end of the lot." Though he wouldn't be able to see it, she pointed to it in the darkness.

"Okay." He lifted Danny into his arms. "Lead the way."

She turned, keeping just one step ahead of them.

"This is getting to be a habit, you know. You carrying Danny for me."

His voice, low so as not to wake Danny, seemed to drift on the spring night air in small, warm waves. "I can think of worse habits."

The problem was, she thought, so could she.

## 9

She had no sooner pulled into her driveway and turned off the engine than she saw Chris walking toward her. He'd arrived just ahead of her and had left his car parked in his driveway. By the time she had unbuckled Danny and gotten out of the car, Chris was at the passenger side.

"I'll take him in," he told her as she opened Danny's door

This time there wasn't even an inclination to protest. It was nice having him around to help. Smiling, Rosemary stepped back and gave Chris clear access to Danny. "I had a hunch that you might."

She left him to pick up her son as she went to unlock the front door. Swinging it open, Rosemary walked in ahead of them. One glance toward the family room told her that Rocky was sleeping peacefully, one paw dipped into her bowl.

Rosemary closed the front door and followed Chris up the stairs. Everything within her was humming.

Chris waited until she joined him at the landing. "Same procedure as last time?"

That had a nice sound to it, she thought. A comfortable sound. She moved past him into Danny's bedroom and pulled back the covers. It was a cool night. She'd cover him with a blanket instead of just a sheet, she decided.

Rosemary nodded in reply to his question. "Shoes and socks, nothing else." She remembered what she had said to Danny earlier this evening. "He might as well be dressed for taking the dog out when he gets up."

Chris laid the boy down. Rosemary took care of one sock and sneaker while Chris took off the other. Very gently, she laid the blanket across Danny's body. He never stirred. Finished, she stood back for a minute, watching Danny as he slept.

She was positively radiant, Chris thought. Motherhood looked very good on her. He found that quality infinitely appealing. And sexy.

"You know," she confided, "it doesn't get much better than this, looking down at your own child, watching him sleep. Knowing he's warm and safe."

A smile quirked Chris's mouth as he placed his hands on her shoulders, peering down at Danny. "Oh, I can think of a few things that might be right up there along with it."

Rosemary froze as she felt his hands move along her shoulders. Not because she didn't want them there, but because she did. She had a sinking feeling that she was just inches away from making a fool of herself in front of him.

They were still the same two people involved, but she had meant what she'd said to Teri. Something seemed to happen when the parameters were altered. When she thought of a man in terms other than a friend. She was headed straight for disaster.

Blowing out a breath, Rosemary eased toward the door. And away from Chris.

She moved onto a safe topic as she walked down the stairs. "You don't have to worry about me making another attempt to set you up with Mary Smith. I think she really missed the boat."

At the bottom of the stairs, Chris turned Rosemary around to face him.

"It hasn't sailed yet." His eyes washed over her, softly whispering along her skin. "In my experience, a solo cruise is a very lonely proposition."

Talk about temptation being right in front of her. Now she had no buffer, no Mary Smith to run interference for her. There was no one to rescue her from making a horrible mistake. Without Mary Smith, she had no client to set him up with. She'd lost her excuse and couldn't refuse going out with him because it wasn't ethical. Chris wasn't really a client, so there was nothing unethical about it.

The nice, easy feeling she'd experienced minutes earlier had dissolved.

Desperate, Rosemary hung on to the conversation like a drowning man to a life preserver. "I mean, according to her profile, the woman was just like me. I wouldn't have stood someone up once, let alone twice." She concentrated on being indignant *for* him instead of attracted *to* him. "I would have found a way to get in contact with you."

In his estimation, he'd been as patient about all this as a man could be. But it couldn't go on indefinitely. "Rosemary?"

She had temporarily run out of steam and paused for a breath. "Yes?"

He cupped his hand along her cheek. "Why don't you give it up?"

She stared at him, though her mouth was dry. What was he talking about? "Give it up? Give what up?"

Just how far did she intend to take this? "The charade."

She realized that he was still touching her. Rosemary pulled away from his hand. She wanted to think clearly. "What charade?"

Obviously, she intended to take this all the way. "You think I haven't figured it out?" He shook his head. "C'mon, Rosemary, give me a little credit."

She was confused. He was accusing her of something and she didn't like it. Defensively, Rosemary placed her hands on her hips. "Well, you can have all the credit you want, but I don't know what you're talking about."

One brow arched in amused disbelief as he looked at her. "Mary Smith?" Chris prodded helpfully.

She still didn't understand his point. "What about her?"

All right, he'd play along. If she wanted him to spell it out for her, he would. Although why she wanted it to go to these lengths was beyond him. "There *is* no Mary Smith."

What was he talking about? Did he actually think that she would have set him up with nobody?

"Of course there's a Mary Smith. I read her letter, I mean, her son's letter." Why did she feel as if she was tripping over her own tongue, as if she was lying? She knew she wasn't. Why did he look as if he knew she was? She felt her honor challenged.

Rosemary drew herself up. All five foot two of her. "Teri said she called the office. She talked to her. Just because Mary Smith didn't show up doesn't mean that she doesn't exist."

As if a bolt of lightning had just streaked across the sky, lighting it up, Rosemary suddenly realized what Chris was getting at. And she didn't like it one bit. She didn't want to believe that Chris actually thought of her as being deceitful and underhanded. Or given to silly mind games the way some women were.

This wasn't a game, this was her work. Her career. It was supposed to be a good deed, damn it. How could it be turning out so badly for her?

Maybe she needed a little time to let go, Chris thought. "Uh-huh."

Her eyes narrowed. "And what does that mean? 'Uh-huh?'"

Chris worded his feelings as tactfully as he could. They'd had a nice time tonight. He didn't want to spoil it with a tissue of a lie any longer.

"It means that I think it's time you stopped pretending."

"Me?" Just what was it that he thought she was pretending about?

"Yes, you." Maybe she did think he was a dolt, and that she could continue this indefinitely. He felt somewhat insulted. "I had a feeling all along that there was no Mary Smith."

"What?" She knew that was what he had been insinuating, but hearing it said aloud made it somehow worse.

He tried changing tactics. Maybe she didn't understand why he had done this. If he had wanted companionship, it would have been a simple enough matter for him to arrange. His voice softened. "I only agreed to be fixed up because I hoped Mary Smith was you. That you were having trouble admitting that you were attracted to me.''

She was staring at him as if he had two heads. Chris felt as if he was losing ground instead of gaining it. ''That for some strange reason you needed this 'familiar' or whatever the hell you wanted to call it, to hide behind in order to make you feel safe. I mean, you did show up every time 'she' didn't. What else was I supposed to think?''

He had to be kidding. Did he actually believe what he was saying? ''That's the most ridiculous thing I've ever heard. Just what are you talking about?''

Enough was enough. How long did she intend to hang on to this threadbare act? ''I don't know. I didn't major in psychology. I'm just taking a stab at it here. All I do know is that I don't want to pretend anymore that she exists.'' It was like trying to go out with ''Sybil'' and having another personality pop up. Rosemary was warm, witty and funny, and he was tired of pretending that he was there to date someone else.

Rosemary didn't get angry, really angry, very often. She was angry now. ''And you think I lied to you.''

He saw the anger in her eyes and reined in his own. He didn't like losing his temper. ''Not lied, exactly. Pretended.''

This was getting worse and worse. "Pretending is for children." She raised her chin. "Are you saying you think I'm a child?"

He didn't want an argument. He just wanted to clear the air. It was turning out to be a great deal more difficult than he had imagined. "I don't know what I think anymore."

"That's obvious if you thought I'd make up someone to go out with you." She strode toward the front door. "I already told you, I don't date." She saw the skepticism on his face. What was it with him? Did he have such a short memory? "I don't feel like being subjected to the agony of defeat, all right?"

*Women should come with instruction books,* he thought ruefully, *even cute, sexy ones. Maybe especially cute sexy ones.* "I didn't see any agony going on tonight. Or last Sunday."

He *did* have a short memory. "That wasn't a date. That was a substitution."

She was one step away from being infuriating. "I don't care what you call it. You can call it Irving for all I care. But it *was* a date." He saw the stubborn glint in her eyes and pressed on. "They both were." Maybe he should have his head examined, but he still wanted to go out with her. Very much. "The first one we had was with your son and your dog. This one was with your son. Can we try it alone next time?"

*Next time?* "No. I mean . . ."

She wavered as temptation flickered through her. But he thought she had lied to him. That she was making all this up. How could he believe such a thing? She'd never do anything like that. He didn't trust her. If that was the way he felt, she didn't want anything to do with him.

"No," she said with a great deal more feeling. "Could you please just leave right now? I don't like being thought of as a liar." He opened his mouth to defend himself, but she cut him off. "I just have to get my head together, all right?"

There was no arguing with her tonight. Maybe he shouldn't have been so abrupt, but damn it, they both knew that he knew. Why did they have to go on with this? "All right. But while you're reconstructing, I want you to think about this."

Before she could protest, or think to protest, Chris pulled her into his arms. In the next heartbeat his mouth was on hers. She felt as if she had tumbled down through a long tunnel.

The next moment she was on that same spiraling roller-coaster ride that she had gotten on the first time. Suddenly she was strapped into a seat, hurtling upside down and backward at breakneck speed into a faraway galaxy.

It was a warm and wonderful place. Frightening and exciting.

His mouth hot on hers, Chris kissed her so hard, so thoroughly, Rosemary didn't think that she would ever come up for air. And maybe that was a good thing. Because where she was was far better than anywhere she'd ever been before. Even if she was upside-down and hurtling backward.

He made her feel like a woman, a woman ripe for loving.

Shaken by what he felt, by what he detected simmering just beneath the surface in her, as well, Chris forced himself to pull back. This wasn't the time to push, no matter what he felt. It was a time for her to reevaluate, to reflect, just as she said. He had to give Rosemary her space.

And maybe get some of his own.

Chris didn't know exactly what was going on here. He did know that he was attracted to her. Damn attracted. And he had the feeling, a very strong feeling, that this could get better. That maybe, just maybe, this could go the distance and that Rosemary Gallagher was that unique, wonderful woman he'd been watching the horizon for. The one with whom, perhaps, he could build his life, a solid life like the one his parents enjoyed.

From the very beginning he'd seen that she wasn't like the others. The women he had dated before Rosemary were all attracted to his looks and to his popularity. Rosemary wasn't like that. She wasn't attracted to superficial things.

If anything, she was fighting her attraction to him. He could sense it, taste it when he kissed her. See it in her eyes.

But it wasn't enough that he felt they had a real chance at something good together. Rosemary had to know it, too.

And it wouldn't do him a damn bit of good to feel the way he did if she didn't know, or wasn't willing to admit the truth.

Truth had to be the cornerstone of their relationship, and at the moment, hormones notwithstanding, it was all looking very shaky.

Resigned for now, he retreated.

"Good night," Chris said as he pulled the door closed behind him.

Rosemary would have said good-night to him if her lips had been in working order. But they weren't. They were completely numb.

And so was she.

She was awake half the night. The other half she spent tossing and turning. Her head was filled with snippets of dreams, all of which ended badly. She was out with Chris, committing the same stupid errors she had on her other two dates. Feeling as if she couldn't do anything right, couldn't think of anything to say.

Each dream ended the same way. With Chris walking out on her.

The last one was so vivid, she woke up with a start. It was six o'clock. Giving up, not wanting to have the same dream again, she remained awake, staring at her digital clock. Waiting for seven and what she deemed was a reasonable hour to call Teri.

Once Teri confirmed that she had spoken to Mary Smith, she could tell Chris to stuff his suspicions and accusations where the sun didn't shine...

When the number flipped to seven on her clock an eternity later, Rosemary pulled the telephone to her and was tapping out Teri's number. She stuffed a pillow behind her, trying to get comfortable.

The phone rang four times.

"C'mon, c'mon, answer," she muttered under her breath. She knew the phone was right by Teri's bed and her cousin liked sleeping in. Jim, an early riser, was probably out jogging somewhere.

Why wasn't she answering?

A sleepy voice mumbled something that sounded close to "Hello?"

Finally! "Teri, it's Rosemary."

"Hmm? Do you know what time it is?"

Impatience drummed through her voice. She wanted to feel vindicated. Now. "It's seven o'clock and if I wanted a confirmation, I would have called the time lady. You have to answer something for me.''

"Can't it wait?''

Teri sounded as if she could fall asleep with the phone in her hand, given half a chance.

"No, Teri,'' Rosemary said urgently, trying to get her to wake up. "It can't.''

She only wanted to ask her if she had spoken to Mary Smith, but instead, the whole story came tumbling out, one word after the other.

"So he thinks I made Mary up and I know you talked to her. All I want you to do is tell me exactly what she said and then I can get back to him and—and tell him to shove it.''

There was a long pause and she thought that Teri had fallen asleep.

"Teri? Answer me.''

Teri sighed. "Are you sitting down?''

She felt a very cool tingling along her spine. "I'm in bed.'' But she rose to her knees. "Why?''

"I didn't talk to Mary Smith.''

That didn't make any sense. Why would Teri say she did when she didn't? "But you said—''

Teri sighed, fully awake now. "I lied.''

Rosemary felt as if she was free-falling from an airplane and her chute refused to open. Earth was coming, spiraling up at her at a maddening speed.

"But why would you say she called if she didn't?" She had an awful feeling she knew the answer to her own question.

"To make you feel a little more confident that she'd show up. Danny was going to take it from there."

"Danny?" She repeated her son's name as if she was suddenly catapulted back into her dream. The name dripped from her lips in slow motion. What did her son have to do with all this?

"Well, yeah." Teri fumbled for words. "Actually, it was Danny's idea." And when he had suggested it, she thought it was wonderful. She still did.

Rosemary felt as if she was locked in a room, trying to find the door in the dark. "You mean, the contest?" She had a feeling that they weren't discussing that.

"Yes, and the letter."

Rosemary's voice dropped to a tense whisper. "What letter?"

There was no use in attempting to keep any of this back. Teri was relieved to finally be able to talk about it. She loved secrets, but she loved telling them even more. Having one and keeping silent wasn't any fun at all.

"Tommy Smith's letter to you. I hate to break it to you, kid, but your son is leading a dual life. He is Tommy Smith. He wrote the letter and I set up a P.O. box so you wouldn't get suspicious. I filled out the form, putting in answers that I knew you would have written."

There was only silence on the other end of the line. Teri began to feel a little nervous. "Oh, c'mon, Rosie, you had to have suspected. We figured you were just playing along with us."

Damn, how stupid could she have been? It was right there in front of her, the perfect match. Tommy was a twin to Danny and Mary was her clone. And she had believed it all.

"No," she said very quietly. "I wasn't." She felt hurt at being duped this way. "I've never done anything underhanded to anyone, so I didn't suspect that it was being done to me. Least of all by my own cousin and my son." Hurt turned into anger. "Damn it, Teri, why would you do such a thing to me?" Chris was right in thinking she was stupid. She was.

Defensiveness sprang to her lips, but then Teri thought better of it. This wasn't about her protecting herself, this was about Rosemary and Rosemary's life.

"For the same reason you set Mary Smith up a second time with Chris." She didn't wait for Rosemary to make a response. "Because you thought she needed prodding. Well, we thought you needed prodding. And you did."

Teri sighed. "I couldn't stand to see Chris Maverick wasted on some bimbo when there you were, absolutely perfect for him."

Rosemary wasn't ready to forgive Teri yet, no matter how good her intentions were. "Why, because I'm breathing?"

Teri gave a short laugh. She loved Rosemary dearly, even if she could be thickheaded at times. "That helps. But that's not the only reason why. You saw it yourself. You have the same interests, and in case you haven't noticed, he's really good with Danny. I knew that would be your first priority in a man. I'm more shallow. Mine would have been drop-dead gorgeous. Mr. Terrific fills both those requirements."

She paused, waiting for Rosemary to say something. When she didn't, some of her confidence faded a little. "Rosie, are you mad at me?"

"Yes." She was struggling hard to hold on to her anger. Teri had no right to meddle like this. But her reasons were good and her heart was in the right place. Rosemary couldn't fault her for that.

Teri was right; Chris *did* have the qualities she would have wanted in a man, but that wasn't the problem. *She* was the problem.

"I only did it because I love you. You deserve to be as happy as the people you're trying so hard to match up."

Rosemary sighed, dragging a hand through her hair. "All right, I forgive you." She frowned, not liking what she had to do next. "I still have to apologize to

Chris. I got on my high horse when he accused me of orchestrating all this myself."

Teri winced, hoping that the damage wasn't too extensive. "Well, you didn't, so you've got a clear conscience."

Yeah, right. "You, dear cousin, obviously have no knowledge of what a clear conscience actually means." Hers was far from clear. "I might not have done this, but it was done because of me, so technically it is my responsibility."

Knowing Rosemary the way she did, Teri realized that she couldn't have expected another reaction. But it could be so damn exasperating at times.

"How many times did your mother take you to see *Pinocchio* as a kid? No, don't answer, whatever it was, it was too much. You OD'd on conscience." Her voice grew serious. "Everything isn't your fault, Rosemary." Teri hunted for an approach that would work for her cousin. "Think of yourself as a guiltless catalyst or something. Unchanged by what transpires around you, yet being the instrument of that transpiration."

"Transpiration?" Rosemary laughed and some of the intensity of her feelings faded. "That's not a word, Teri."

"No, it's not," she agreed. "It's a feeling. Right now, I feel that you and Chris should be together. So does Danny. So does Chris if I don't miss my guess, since he went along with it, according to you, thinking that Mary Smith was a pseudonym for you. Three brilliant people can't be wrong. Especially if one of those people looks great in a thong."

She knew Teri's wardrobe as well as her own. "You don't own one."

"No, but if you're lucky, he does."

Rosemary could hear the wide grin in Teri's voice. "I have to go now, Teri. Thanks to you and Danny, I have to eat humble pie."

It was a trade-off. "As long as you cleanse your palate with him."

According to Teri, the whole thing was a done deal. But she had said a lot of things last night, had been very self-righteously angry. She wasn't so sure it would be a bridge she could reconstruct. And she suddenly knew she wanted to. Very much.

"You're impossible."

"Yeah, but I'm lovable. Go get him, Rosemary." Her voice softened, filled with affection. "Don't let all this be for naught."

She wasn't sure she caught the drift of what Teri was driving at now. "What 'all this'?"

Not only did she have to lead this horse to water, she had to stick the straw in it for her, too. "Well, you dated him, didn't you?"

That was what Chris had said yesterday. But technically, in her mind, it hadn't been a date either time. "No, I—"

"All right, you were anesthetized by thinking that this woman would pop up eventually, but the fact is that you did go out with him and you did have a terrific time by your own admission. At the very least, that should show you something."

"That I do well in a group." Rosemary swung her legs off the edge of the bed. "I always knew that."

"All right, take a bunch of hand puppets in your purse. Or gerbils if it makes you feel better. Just don't let this guy get away."

Far easier said than done. The damage she'd done might be beyond her power to fix. "I yelled at him for calling me a liar, Teri. I think he's already gone."

"His kind has far greater staying power than you're giving him credit for. Apologize and take it from there."

"I—"

"*Apologize and take it from there,*" Teri repeated firmly.

Rosemary pressed her lips together. It was the only path open to her. Even if she didn't want to make a stab at a relationship beyond being friends with him, she had to apologize for what she'd said. And she still wanted Chris to know that she didn't have anything to do with the charade.

"We'll see," Rosemary said as she hung up.

"I sincerely hope so," Teri whispered to herself as she replaced the telephone.

# *10*

━━━◆━━━

Three hours later, when Rosemary walked up Chris's driveway, it felt as if she was walking the last mile before her execution. She was definitely *not* looking forward to this, but one way or another, it had to be done.

She would have called him if she could, but she didn't have his phone number. There was no Chris Maverick in the white pages of her telephone book and Information said he was unlisted.

That left only one way open to her if she was going to resolve things.

Face-to-face made it a great deal more difficult. But she owed him an apology and she wasn't the kind to let things like that slide.

Maybe she *had* seen *Pinocchio* one too many times, she thought ruefully as she rang his bell.

She hoped he was in. She didn't want to go through the agony of psyching herself up again later. As it was, it had taken her the entire time she'd driven Danny to his friend's house and then back to work up her courage to do this.

Danny had been very quiet and contrite after the dressing-down she had given him. But in the end, she'd forgiven him just as she had Teri. He meant well. Still, she had extracted a promise from him that he was never going to try to do something so secretive again.

That should last until he was in his teens, she judged.

Her palms felt wet. She didn't mind admitting she was wrong; she just hated the embarrassment that went along with it.

When he didn't answer, she rang again. She knew he was home. This was Saturday and he didn't have a radio show to do. Besides, his car was still in the driveway where he'd left it last night.

There was still no answer. Rosemary leaned on the bell.

"Please, answer," she muttered under her breath. "And let me get this over with."

The door was suddenly yanked open. Startled, Rosemary took a step backward before the sight of Chris registered in her brain.

He was standing dripping in the doorway, a black terry-cloth towel wrapped around his hips, another draped over his sleek shoulders.

Déjà vu.

Except that this time he looked far from happy.

Chris rubbed one end of the towel over his wet head, his eyes fixed on hers.

"Is there some kind of a warning system hooked up to my shower?" he demanded. "Does it go off whenever I turn on the water and leave you with an uncontrollable desire to come running over and ring my doorbell?"

If this was going to be done, she had to do it quickly. Pulling back would only make her lose her momentum and her courage. Holding on to both, she pushed past Chris and walked into the house.

"Kind of testy today, aren't we?"

He stared at her. What was she doing here? After last night he'd figured that maybe things needed to cool off between them before they spoke to each other again. She'd certainly given him that impression.

"I always get that way after I'm made to feel as if I'm the bad guy. It's my way of working it out of my system."

And trying to work *her* out of his system, as well. Sometime last night he'd come to the realization that maybe he was butting his head against a brick wall with her. That maybe she was serious about not wanting a romantic relationship with him or with anyone. If that was the way she really felt, then pushing could only be construed as being obsessive.

So he'd decided to back off. And here she was, ringing his bell and his chimes. It certainly didn't make things easier for him.

Rosemary wished he was wearing something other than that towel again. The first time she'd seen him this way, it had unnerved her. And that was before he'd kissed her. Now she felt as if there were ants all over her body, moving insistently along, tingling her skin.

She looked at his wet hair and hoped her eyes would stay put. The sight of the rest of him was a bit more than she could calmly endure.

"I came over to apologize."

Chris stopped toweling his hair and looked at her. "Oh?"

She faced him squarely, drawing herself up. "But it's not what you think."

He cocked his head, studying her. She seemed full of confidence and nervous at the same time. He couldn't help hoping the latter was because of him. "Then tell me what to think."

She wanted him to believe her in the worst way. "I really didn't know about the Mary Smith thing. I honestly thought I was setting you up with someone. Maybe I'm stupid, but I just don't think in those kinds of terms."

He shook his head. She was leaving something out. "What terms? You've lost me."

*Just as long as you don't lose that towel, we're okay.*
"Devious ones." She perched on the arm of his over-stuffed sofa. "Teri and Danny set me up." She licked her lips. God, but they felt dry. "They set both of us up, really. Except that you caught on." She couldn't help the small accusing look that came into her eyes. "Sort of."

He took her hands in his and pulled her to her feet. Rosemary could feel the body heat radiating between them. And a yearning budding in hers.

"Can we back up here for a minute? Are you telling me that you didn't know that there was no Mary Smith? That you weren't the one to make her up?"

He was still skeptical, she thought, and it bothered her.

"That's what I'm telling you." She frowned. It was a no-win situation. If he didn't believe her, he'd think she was lying. If he did believe her, he'd probably think she was an idiot. "That doesn't make me exactly a rocket scientist, does it?"

He could afford to smile. She hadn't been devious. It was the one thing that hadn't clicked before. Devious didn't seem to suit her personality. He felt relieved. And incredibly turned on, standing here in a towel, with her scent wafting to him.

"Oh, I don't know." He threaded his fingers through her hair. "I never went out with a rocket scientist myself. Something tells me, though, that they get so wrapped up in their work, they miss a few signs, too." He pressed a kiss to her temple.

Suddenly she was finding it very difficult to breathe. "You're being nice about this, but I feel badly."

"Why?" He nipped her lips slightly, barely touching them. Exciting himself—and her, he hoped. "I had a great time, I already told you." He stopped for a second to look into her eyes. "Unless you didn't."

"No, I did." He feathered a kiss along her jawline and her mouth almost fell open. She was having more and more difficulty pushing the words out of her mouth. "It's just that, well, it's the way I told you." Her limbs were on their way to permanent liquefaction. "On a date, I become a mindless idiot."

"I doubt that." He felt her pulse leap in her throat as he skimmed his lips along it. "All right, we won't date."

"We won't?" She was holding on to his shoulders now to keep from slipping away. Or maybe to keep him from stopping.

His words brought her around. He was saying what she wanted him to say. At least, what she had thought she wanted him to say. But now that he did, something within her was screaming *no*.

"No, we won't," he repeated. "I have a better idea. We'll hang out together." She'd said that being friends had made her feel more comfortable with her late husband. Then that was the route to go. "In different places. Just like friends."

She could feel every rippling muscle, every nuance of his desire. "What kind of friends?"

"Close friends," he whispered along her shoulder.

She could hardly swallow, but then, that didn't seem very important at the moment. Her mouth curved. "How close?"

He looked into her eyes, his own glinting with mischief. And desire. "Close enough that if my towel starts to slip, you'd grab it for me and hold it up." He sealed his arms around her.

Rosemary felt something wild and wicked and wonderfully free being released within her. "How high would you want me to hold it?"

He outlined the shape of her earlobe with his tongue and she was sinking at a speed that could only be measured in light-years.

"I was thinking of somewhere over your head. But don't let me rush you." Tracing a path with his mouth, he switched to her other ear. "Take all the time you want."

She was melting into his arms, he could feel it, although no faster than he was dissolving himself. But a thought suddenly burst on his brain, bringing everything to a temporary halt.

"Where's Danny?"

Danny? Oh, her son. Right. "I drove him to his friend's house." Thank God she'd had the presence of mind to think of that. She'd done it to keep him from seeing his mother eat crow, not because she'd expected to unlock the door of paradise. "He'll be gone all afternoon."

Chris framed Rosemary's face in his hands. "And the dog?"

That one took her a second longer to remember. "Sleeping."

His smile began in his eyes and reached down to his lips. "Then we're alone."

"Yes." Rosemary was barely aware of mouthing the word.

He kissed each eyelid shut and felt her heart hammering against his chest. "And it looks as if we're going to stay that way for a while."

"Yes."

"Perfect."

He found her mouth a second before she was going to pull him toward it. The kiss was wild, exciting, and just rough enough around the edges to show her what lay in store. And what it was that she had nearly backed away from.

Her head spinning madly, Rosemary pulled her lips from his. "Chris?"

"Hmm?" He didn't want to talk anymore. It was past the time for words. He kissed her again.

"Your towel's slipping." Her mouth curved against his in a smile.

"I think you know what to do."

She grinned wickedly. "Yes, I do. I know exactly what to do."

His eyes held hers as they darkened with a passion that he had bridled until now. The very look excited her beyond words.

"Then do it."

She held her breath. Her heart pounded anyway. "With no dog to blame it on?"

Very slowly he moved his head from side to side. "I don't think we need any familiars running interference any longer."

"No," she agreed as her fingers curved along the perimeter of the towel, the portion that was just below his navel. "We don't."

The black terry-cloth towel blended very well with the gray carpeting that it landed on. Which was just as well. Because it remained there, unnoticed, for a very, very long time.

\*　　\*　　\*　　\*　　\*

"Motherhood is full of love, laughter
and sweet surprises. Silhouette's collection
is every bit as much fun!"
—Bestselling author Ann Major

This May, treat yourself to...

# WANTED:

Silhouette's annual tribute to motherhood takes a
new twist in '96 as three sexy single men prepare for
fatherhood—and saying "I Do!" This collection makes
the perfect gift, not just for moms but for all romance
fiction lovers! Written by these captivating authors:

## Annette Broadrick
## Ginna Gray
## Raye Morgan

"The Mother's Day anthology from Silhouette is the
highlight of any romance lover's spring!"
—Award-winning author **Dallas Schulze**

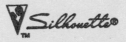

In July, get to know the Fortune family....

Next month, don't miss the start of Fortune's Children, a
fabulous new twelve-book series from Silhouette Books.

**Meet the Fortunes**—a family whose legacy is greater than
riches. Because where there's a will...there's a wedding!

When Kate Fortune's plane crashes in the jungle, her family
believes that she's dead. And when her will is read, they
discover that Kate's plans for their lives are more interesting
than they'd ever suspected.

Look for the first book, *Hired Husband,* by *New York Times*
bestselling author Rebecca Brandewyne. PLUS, a stunning,
perforated bookmark is affixed to *Hired Husband* (and
selected other titles in the series), providing a convenient
checklist for all twelve titles!

**FREE**
Keepsake
Bookmark

Launching in July wherever books are sold.

## MILLION DOLLAR SWEEPSTAKES
## AND EXTRA BONUS PRIZE DRAWING

# Silhouette's recipe for a sizzling summer:

* Take the best-looking cowboy in South Dakota
* Mix in a brilliant bachelor
* Add a sexy, mysterious sheikh
* Combine their stories into one collection and you've got one sensational super-hot read!

*Summer Sizzlers*

**MEN OF Summer**

Three short stories by these favorite authors:

## Kathleen Eagle
## Joan Hohl
## Barbara Faith

Available this July wherever
Silhouette books are sold.

# This July, watch for the delivery of...

An exciting new miniseries that appears in a different Silhouette series each month. It's about love, marriage—and Daddy's unexpected need for a baby carriage!

Daddy Knows Last unites five of your favorite authors as they weave five connected stories about baby fever in New Hope, Texas.

- **THE BABY NOTION** by Dixie Browning
  (SD#1011, 7/96)

- **BABY IN A BASKET** by Helen R. Myers
  (SR#1169, 8/96)

- **MARRIED...WITH TWINS!**
  by Jennifer Mikels
  (SSE#1054, 9/96)

- **HOW TO HOOK A HUSBAND (AND A BABY)**
  by Carolyn Zane
  (YT#29, 10/96)

- **DISCOVERED: DADDY** by Marilyn Pappano
  (IM#746, 11/96)

Daddy Knows Last arrives in July...only from

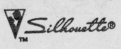

DKLT

# You're About to Become a

## *Privileged Woman*

Reap the rewards of fabulous free gifts and benefits with proofs-of-purchase from Silhouette and Harlequin books

# Pages & Privileges™

It's our way of thanking you for buying our books at your favorite retail stores.

**PROOF OF PURCHASE**
Offer expires October 31, 1996
YT-PP137

Pages & Privileges ™

**Harlequin and Silhouette—
the most privileged readers in the world!**

For more information about Harlequin and Silhouette's PAGES & PRIVILEGES program call the Pages & Privileges Benefits Desk: 1-503-794-2499

*Silhouette*®

YT-PP137